THE
LAST
MYSTERY
OF
EDGAR
ALLAN
POE

D1547247

THE LAST MYSTERY OF EDGAR ALLAN POE

THE TROY DOSSIER

MANNY MEYERS

J. B. Lippincott Company · Philadelphia and New York

Copyright © 1978 by Manny Meyers, Ph.D.
All rights reserved
First edition
2 4 6 8 9 7 5 3 1

Printed in the United States of America

U.S. Library of Congress Cataloging in Publication Data

Meyers, Manny, birth date
The last mystery of Edgar Allan Poe.

1.   Poe, Edgar Allan, 1809–1849, in fiction, drama,
poetry, etc. I. Title.
PZ4.M6146Las [PS3563E94] 813′.5′4   78–17283
ISBN–0–397–01315–9

To my son, Jonathan, age four
From his innocence, joy
May he excel

THE
LAST
MYSTERY
OF
EDGAR
ALLAN
POE

Prologue

JANUARY 1845

SOMEWHERE IN EUROPE

"Over here. Do be careful. It is difficult to see and any disturbance would be dangerous. You have kept us waiting. . . ."

"I am most sorry, your—"

"Please, no salutations! Hardly a place for an audience, but it is necessary for this occasion. We chose this place partly because no one would ever believe us capable of descending to these undercellars. Let us therefore remain only for the minimal time required.

"There will be no interruption. The corridors are long and narrow, and voices are clearly audible for distances. If there were the slightest indication of our presence here there would be consequences. Therefore, you are enjoined to be brief in your comments, should any be essential.

"Your proposal has been read. It has substantial merit, and it is, though exceedingly bold, most plausible. True, it is fraught with potential hazard to this country, and somewhat lesser danger to our personage. Yet its failure would hardly bring about our downfall, and its success would fulfill God's beneficent design. Thus, it is our decision to sponsor your undertaking.

"There will be stringent qualifications, of course. There can be no official sanction of this venture. Should you be exposed at any time before the final phase is put into execution, your fate will be in your own hands. Obversely, should you bring this plan to the penultimate stage successfully, you have our word that the final step will be set in motion no matter what the cost.

"You will be financed from our private purse. And although we desire to be informed periodically of your progress, the secrecy of this project must be retained at all costs.

"There must be a cover of immunity which will ensure that your messages reach our eyes exclusively. There is a way to do this. A most entertaining story was read to me the other day. The author is, amazingly, an American. Its theme is that when one wishes to hide an item, the best method is to display it prominently, for this will be the least likely place the seeker will think to look. Therefore, our secretary will be instructed to carry your communiqués directly to our person. The correspondence must seem to be of a personal nature, yet contain some sort of code which would alert him to bring this to our express attention. Let us think of something distinctive.

"Do you know classical history? Most pertinent would be a story wherein the lesser vies with the greater: the rivalry of Rome and Carthage or the Greeks with the Trojans. Yes, Troy would be most apropos. Any agent or communication bearing the designation Troy will receive our instant and confidential attention. This interview is at an end. Now the episode begins."

1

DECEMBER 1846

NEW YORK CITY
(City Hall and Chatham Street)
AND FORDHAM VILLAGE

"Is there not enough insanity in this situation without you adding more? Your proposal is unadulterated madness, and I will not permit it. I refuse, I absolutely refuse." The Mayor of New York City, James Harper, punctuated each phrase with the emphatic gesture of his right arm as he paced the length of his huge desk.

"Nevertheless I require it," replied Hollis Beckwith, the Police Superintendent. He was gazing out the double window of the City Hall south toward Park Row. In the darkness of early morning he could barely see the gothic tower of Trinity Church.

"Hollis, Hollis," Harper protested, "you and I have been working together for two years now. Your future is tied with mine. Do you want to ruin both of us?"

"I require it," Beckwith repeated without turning around.

"If this gets out, and it surely will, the City of New York will be laughed at all over these twenty-eight states and beyond the Continental Divide. Is that what you want? Don't we have enough trouble now with the two murdered girls? And not just ordinary girls, mind you, but daughters of the best Knickerbocker society. Families with power and influence enough to lift me right out of the Mayor's chair if they decide to go against me."

"Nevertheless I require it."

"Goddammit, you sound like the refrain from the necromancer's latest scribbling: *Nevermore, nevermore, nevermore.* Hollis, do you realize what you are asking? This Poe has a bad reputation—and I am not talking about his literary one. He is a drunkard, an incorrigible troublemaker, a womanizer, and an opium eater. He dabbles in all sorts of un-Christian things. Two young girls are hideously murdered, and your remedy is to consult this malignant poet."

"I understand what you say, but I want Edgar Allan Poe to assist me in the solution of these murders."

Harper stared at him and suddenly capitulated. "Hollis, if I were not aware of your capabilities I would fling you pell-mell from my office. But you are shrewd and politic, and for a man in a most difficult position, you have a superb record. If you insist upon having Edgar Allan Poe to assist you in these horrors, I will not stand in your way. But remember one thing: The entire responsibility is yours. If anything goes awry, despite all you have done for my administration, I will discharge you faster than you can write your resignation."

Beckwith said nothing. He had no wish to antagonize the Mayor, a good man but one who easily yielded to pressure. He could not reveal his plan, which even he had to admit was a gamble. Besides, he had already gone too far by suppressing certain details of both murders from everyone. As he walked out of the Mayor's office, Harper's voice bellowed from behind the desk, "You want the dissolute Mr. Poe, you shall have the dissolute Mr. Poe, but he will not receive one cent of city funds." Beckwith did not tell him that he had already anticipated this.

The first Police Superintendent of New York City walked down the twelve stone steps of the City Hall and veered right on Broadway toward his office in the Old Jail building on Chatham Street.

There was much to do: reports to be completed, inspections to be made, questions to be asked, and investigators to be assigned. With luck, he could keep the details of the second crime from the newspapers, particularly the despicable penny press. Their stories about the first murder had taken almost all their column space for three days. There had not been such excitement about a crime in New York since Mary Cecilia Rogers, a beautiful countergirl at John Anderson's tobacco shop on Nassau Street, was brutally strangled in November 1841.

The second murder was sure to increase the fear in a city which was already afraid when darkness came. Homicides were expected, but it was quite another thing to have a wily maniac loose in the metropolis. Beckwith wanted everything to be functioning efficiently when he left office. Without the murders, in another eight months he could have a police system in operation which no man could disrupt without difficulty. He must temporarily lay aside that goal to concentrate on capturing the Garroter.

It was not the first time Beckwith had staked his all. Speculation was part of his nature. That was what he savored about any venture. The novel, the unexpected, the problematical—to take it all within his grasp and mold it as he directed.

The Beckwiths had always taken risks, as far back as the family history could be traced. Rebelling against a tyrannical Puritan oligarchy, his great-grandfather had departed a Congregational settlement north of Boston and moved across western Massachusetts into upper New York State, settling on land near Utica. His father became the proprietor of the general store. The opening of the Erie Canal brought a boom to the area.

His father's prosperity had allowed Hollis to go beyond the education usually provided for a young man of his station. When there were not enough books in all of Oneida County to satisfy him, his father hired itinerant tutors to supplement his education. Six months before the end of Andrew Jackson's second term, the family decided to move with the western migration. The sale of the Utica property brought $75,000 in specie which held its value in the Panic of 1837. The other Beckwiths were now prospering in Fort Wayne, Indiana, on the Wabash and Erie Canal. Hollis was in New York City.

Long before, he had joined the Utica Municipal Democratic Party, most of whose members were left over from the days when the aristocratic DeWitt Clinton was in power. In the minority, Beckwith declared himself with the Martin Van Buren bloc, which subsequently took over the Democratic Party apparatus. So thorough was the dapper, diminutive Van Buren's control that he had himself elected to the U. S. Senate and left the affairs of New York State to a group of men loyal to him. This political directorate was dubbed the Albany Regency.

As a reward for his political acumen and loyalty, Beckwith became executive secretary of the Albany Regency, privy to all its proceedings. He was just beginning to be bored with that job when he learned that the Democratic mayor of New York City needed someone to head the first full-time municipal police force in the Union. Beckwith asked for the position.

It was four o'clock in the afternoon before Beckwith was able to leave his office after his early morning meeting with the Mayor. Poe lived in Fordham village, some thirteen miles north. Beckwith had hired a horse and ridden off in the gathering darkness.

The day had been cold. Now, at dusk, the only light was an irregular slit of glaring orange glazed over by a lackluster bluish gray edging the western horizon. Beckwith wished he had started earlier. It was growing increasingly bitter. He was almost numb when he saw the light.

In the distance it appeared as if the house was precariously set on the crest of a wave and would be dashed to pieces on the ground below at any moment. As he drew closer, Beckwith realized that the house did perch on the precipice of a concave hill and it was possible that a gale might overturn it.

He directed the horse toward a semicircular path. Closer now, he could make out the shingled roof with a chimney at one end, sloped steeply to the wide upper windows.

There was a weighted stillness about the house. He tied his horse, went to the door, and knocked. There was a long pause. Had he made the long trip for nothing? He had raised his hand to knock again when the door opened. Her size surprised him. She seemed to fill the small doorway.

"Good evening, ma'am. Is this the residence of Mr. Edgar Allan Poe?"

"What is your business, sir?" Her voice was not unpleasant, but she appeared determined not to move unless the answer satisfied her.

Beckwith's response was to hand her his card, which she held high to catch the candlelight. She flushed as she read the words.

"Mr. Poe is ill," she stated.

"I am sorry to hear that," he said gently. "I wish to discuss a situation with him, one which I am sure would profit him." Her blunt features could not disguise her relief.

"Yes, Mr. Poe is ill, but he is recuperating rapidly," she amended. "I know he would be interested in any project with remuneration." The last two words were unabashedly emphasized.

"That is exactly the type of enterprise I had in mind," he articulated.

"Please come in. If you like I will take your coat, although I recommend you keep it on. I am Mrs. Maria Clemm. Mr. Poe is my nephew as well as being married to my daughter."

Beckwith took off his greatcoat. He realized at once that it would have been better to keep it on, for the house was exceedingly cold.

"You had better come warm yourself at the fireplace," Mrs. Clemm said. She was insulated by her heavy clothing and had evidently become inured to freezing temperatures. As she led him into another small room, he noticed that her hazel eyes were alert to his every movement.

There was hardly any furniture—a chair, a table, some other mismatched pieces. Their circumstances, it took no brilliant feat of detection to work out, were those of extreme privation. How could this be? Beckwith wondered. As the author of "The Raven," Poe's name was on everyone's lips from Boston to

Charleston. There are many subjects on which I am ignorant, thought Beckwith, and assuredly writing as a profession is one of them. In the room to which Mrs. Clemm led him was a bed, close to the fireplace, in which lay a young woman. She was covered with five or six blankets; at her feet was a large black cat.

"This is my daughter, Virginia, wife to Mr. Poe," Mrs. Clemm said. "And our cat, Catarina. She has been with us since Richmond days." The girl's pale face looked in his direction, but her lips did not move.

"Forgive her, Mr. Beckwith. Virginia has been ill for a long time and is very weak. Now I will see if Mr. Poe will receive you."

Beckwith stood sideways to the fire, not wishing to obstruct, even slightly, the current of heated air from its source to the bed.

A few moments later Mrs. Clemm returned and indicated that he was to follow her. She led him to a tiny staircase. Everything in the cottage seemed diminutive. Up they went, to what seemed more an attic than a second floor. She knocked, paused, and opened the door.

In the light of a solitary candle, Beckwith could see a man lying in a narrow bed. He was propped up by a pillow. His face was so white it blended into the linen.

2

DECEMBER 1846

FORDHAM VILLAGE

"Come in, sir," the writer said in a low voice. "Muddie, please, another candle. I am afraid our guest is not as acclimated to this poor light as we are."

Mrs. Clemm had anticipated the request. She was already setting in a second holder the candle she had used to guide Beckwith upstairs. Without another word, she closed the door.

There was now a candle on each side of Poe's bed. To Beckwith the setting was theatrically funereal. Then he studied the other man's face and noted something singular about the eyes: the poet's pupils were pinpoints. In this light, the pupils should be enlarged. It would be the effect of the drugs, he realized.

"Have I the honor of addressing Edgar Allan Poe?" Beckwith inquired decorously.

"It is an honor only if you deem it an honor, sir," said the other with a faint smile.

Beckwith winced inwardly. His report had stated that the poet was susceptible to flattery. Obviously, Poe was either in ill health or ill humor or that type of flattery was ineffective. In any case, Beckwith would not make the same mistake again.

"I would offer you something to drink," continued the author, "but liquor is not permitted in this house. I would offer you a seat, sir, only there is none."

"Mr. Poe, I have come here to—" Before Beckwith could complete the sentence, the poet interrupted.

"You have come on a matter of the greatest urgency," Poe said. "Specifically, you have come to request my assistance to solve what will undoubtedly be dubbed the 'Garroter murders.' For the second one, I fear, took place within the past twenty-four hours."

"Precisely, Mr. Poe," replied Beckwith, nonplussed by the man's incisiveness, but managing to retain his impassive expression. "How do you know this?"

"You are the Police Superintendent of the City of New York. You took the exceptional course of riding thirteen miles on a bitter evening. Therefore, an exceptional crime has occurred. What, sir, has been the universal topic in the metropolis these past two months but the garroting of Angelina Van Cortlandt?"

"How could you be aware of her murder?" Beckwith inquired. "You have been seriously ill since October."

"Miss Van Cortlandt was killed the day before I became sick," the writer responded. "So I knew about it. As for the public's reaction, it is apparent from those publications." Poe pointed to a dim corner at the right of his bed where newspapers and magazines were stacked.

"No, I could not afford to buy them," said Poe, again correctly divining his guest's thoughts. "They are gratuitous exchange copies, one to two months old. The last mementos, besides my debts, of my ownership of the *Broadway Journal*. But to return to the main topic. You, the Police Superintendent, are in my home. So I hypothesize that there has been another garroting of a young girl.

"Yes, yes," Poe reiterated, as if saying it aloud helped to affirm the validity of his reasoning. "It would have to be in replicated circumstances. If it were a different crime, you would not resort to the extraordinary measure of coming here. A certain time had to pass for you to concede your inability to cope with

18

the first murder and your helplessness when faced with a second and similar one."

Beckwith started. This was unexpected. He would have to be cautious to keep the poet from knowing his real purpose, for the man was as acute in his observations as in his writings. He endeavored to gain control.

"Marvelous, Mr. Poe, simply marvelous," Beckwith said, though he kept an even tone. His admiration was sincere, but it must not be overdone. "I see I have come to the right person."

This time the flattery worked. There was a glimmer in Poe's somber eyes and his thin lips relaxed.

"Everything you deduce is correct," confirmed the Police Superintendent. "My purpose here is to request your assistance to apprehend a most brutal murderer."

The figure in the bed was immobile. Such was the silence that when the wick of the candle bent and the flame touched the hot wax the sibilant sound was clearly heard.

"But there is more involved than the capture of a homicidal maniac," Beckwith went on. "As you must know, the City of New York is experimenting with a municipal police force, on the British model. I took the assignment of Police Superintendent probably with the same misgivings as those with which Sir Robert Peel, the innovator of the English police force, must have taken his. Yet it is a challenge to which I am fully committed. I mean that in every sense of the word, for my reputation is at stake."

"Then you are most assuredly a gentleman, sir," Poe enunciated.

Beckwith ignored the unintended condescension clothed in the compliment. "The murder of Angelina Van Cortlandt was a shocking affair. Now add to that the garroting of Alicia Schuyler last night."

"Alicia Schuyler!" exclaimed Poe. "My God, she was such a vivacious creature."

"You knew her then?"

"I was acquainted with both girls," Poe answered softly,

19

stunned by the news. "They regularly attended my literary readings."

"Then you know that both victims were members of two of the most powerful families in New York State. Their fathers will use their influence to dismantle my Star Police if there is no success in solving these murders. Mr. Poe, there is inordinate pressure upon Mayor Harper and myself."

"Ah, my friend James Harper, the publisher turned politician," the author muttered facetiously. Some years before Poe had proposed to Harper & Brothers the publication of a volume of his prose works; the venture was aborted and there were still hard feelings on both sides.

"Yet I will not pick the first likely suspect and accuse him," Beckwith declared, "either to satisfy the whims of the public or to mollify these distinguished families. Firstly, it would be reprehensible to accuse without certainty. Secondly, it would be a travesty to convict without evidence. Thirdly, it would do no good in any case should I acquiesce to these pressures."

"Why is that, Mr. Beckwith?" the poet asked. "In my studies of cases verité, I have found that the expeditious technique is conviction by circumstantial evidence."

"Because, Mr. Poe," Beckwith retorted with a pomposity he had not intended, "there may be inept prosecutors, but I am not an incompetent policeman. Also, if I had an accused man in jail and there was another garroting, there would be no need for me to resign, I would probably be ridiculed out of my position. That is why I need your help."

"I am bewildered, sir," Poe said, feigning puzzlement. "I am a writer of poetry, prose, and criticism, a student of languages, mathematics, and the physical sciences. I have no experience in police work."

"You deprecate your own talents, Mr. Poe, for I find you eminently qualified to aid me in this matter. Let us go back a step. I am dealing not only with a new organization but with a new type of criminal behavior, unrecorded on the North American continent. Let me give further details. My investigation thus far has revealed that these two murders were elaborately executed, yet there appears to be no motive. What kind of homicidal personality am I dealing with? In all candor, Mr. Poe, I am uncertain. Therefore, I must apply new techniques to this novel situation. I can perhaps state my attitude with this perverse principle: the application of the intellect to the irrational.

"You, Mr. Poe, are a pioneer in modern crime detection. It is a matter of life following art, for the manifesto for this contemporary approach, as far as I am concerned, dates from the publication of 'The Murders in the Rue Morgue' in 1843. This revolutionary exposition I now restate."

The Police Superintendent pulled out of his right inside jacket pocket a sheaf of folded papers.

"I quote from your C. Auguste Dupin: *'The necessary knowledge is that of what to observe. . . . We must not judge of the means,' said Dupin, 'by this shell of an examination. The Parisian police, so much extolled for acumen, are cunning, but no more. There is no method in their proceedings, beyond the method of the moment.'* "

"Please, Mr. Beckwith, there is no need to recite my theories; I am quite familiar with them," said Poe irascibly.

"Very well, I was merely highlighting the portions which attracted me. Applying all the variables in a case in their proper perspective, no more and no less than needed—that is the paramount ratiocinative principle, as I see it. And that lovely word you use to describe crimes which require the intellect for resolution," Beckwith continued, in an almost rhapsodic tone. *"Disentanglement.* How precise, how poetic."

He paused. Were his words having their meant effect? In this still moment he heard the wood creak just beyond the door. It was of no consequence. Let her listen.

"There is another factor in this disentanglement. Note that I do not use the plural, Mr. Poe, for, despite the two murders, this is a *singular* case. There is a cryptogram involved, if that is what

21

one can label it. And you are the acknowledged master of the cryptogram. I know that you issued a challenge that there was not a code you could not decipher. You have been successful in solving all. And you were correct when you pronounced some of them nonsensical gibberish designed merely to frustrate you. There is none who can best you at this."

"I wish to heaven I had never issued that confounded cryptogram challenge," Poe broke in. "It was foolish vanity which wasted my time and profited me nothing. And it is in this vein I say, Mr. Beckwith, that I regret any inconvenience that you suffered in coming here, but you have wasted your time. I will not do it, sir, I absolutely refuse. I would not accept this task if all the hounds of Hell were after me."

"But, Mr. Poe, I am desperate."

"As you are here, sir, and are aware of my circumstances, you are not the only one who is desperate."

"I see, Mr. Poe. You think that I wish your services gratis. It would be an interesting challenge, would it not?"

"Challenges weary me, Mr. Beckwith." The resignation in the poet's voice accentuated the point. "I am challenged, I perform, I overcome, and I am left with nothing. I have proved myself to myself and am no longer interested in the world's acclaim. Renown has brought me to this: continual ill health and exposure to these bitter Fordham nights, unable to provide sustenance for my two dependents—"

"I am sorry, Mr. Poe, I intended to introduce the matter of emoluments Monday at my office."

"I cannot wait for Monday. For if your *emoluments* are unsuitable, it would profit me more to go into the woods and chop some firewood come the sunrise."

"Very well, I am prepared to discuss arrangements. The Van Courtlandt family has offered five hundred dollars for the apprehension of the murderer of their daughter." This was Beckwith's first enticement.

"Five hundred dollars is a paltry sum for such a wealthy

family," Poe retorted. "As an editor for four months I would earn an equal amount."

Beckwith knew little of the pay of editors, but he did know Poe was exaggerating his recompense. However, he had no wish to contest the poet at this time. Ignoring the remark, he added, "The Schuyler family will probably offer more for the capture of the killer of their daughter. I am hopeful it will be a thousand dollars, certainly a minimum of seven hundred and fifty."

"I agree, Mr. Beckwith. The Schuylers were never afflicted with morality in the making of their fortune; thus they can be generous in dispensing it."

"There you have it, an assured five hundred dollars, another probable sum of a thousand or more. That is about a year's salary for you."

"Then I refuse, categorically refuse."

"For what reason? It is a quite considerable total." Beckwith could not allow this project to fail.

"It is a considerable amount, as you say. However, there is one basic fallacy to this proposition."

"And that is?"

"Mr. Beckwith, you importune me to accept this grand offer on the grounds I will be successful—an assurance I cannot give myself, much less you. Let us then proceed on the basis that the worst will happen to me—as it usually does. Here I interpolate an incident which will show you how fate favors me. In November, just after 'The Raven' was published, I arranged a reading of my poetry at the Winter Garden. That hall had never experienced such an advance sale. It was an assured sell-out, and the fee would have supported me for six months. That day a storm such as has seldom been seen struck the city—all the varieties of frozen precipitation as could be conjured up by an outraged shaman. The advance had to be returned and I have not been able to reschedule it.

"Suppose I fail to find your murderer. What compensation do I receive? Nothing. But if I do not commit myself to this enterprise, I have some stories meandering through my mind that I could complete.

"Also, what you ask me to undertake is an actuality—real murders and real victims. I salute the challenge, I eschew the danger. However, in fiction I control what is happening: I can create success. In life I have not that power. I am not so immersed in my own fantasies that failure can be dismissed. Indeed, if I had such delusions, all I need do is to look about me or to review my life."

Beckwith relaxed; his stratagem was working. The poet was responding as he wished. Poe must believe that the offer was a result of his own hard bargaining.

"You are quite right. Certainly one does not ask an attorney to take a case with the prerequisite that he win or summon a physician on the condition that the patient will recover. Both receive a fee no matter the outcome. Let me think a moment. . . . Is this satisfactory? While I am not a wealthy man, I have an independent income. From my private funds I will pay you one hundred and fifty dollars whether or not you succeed in this enterprise. Further, I will renounce the reward should our joint efforts lead to the solution; you may have it all."

"And the period and conditions this retainer covers?"

"Your services at my full-time disposal for three months, at the end of which time we will renegotiate the terms," Beckwith said. "Further, I will pay your expenses at the rate of two dollars a day for the first month, one and a half for the second month and one dollar for the third month."

"Two dollars a day," a buoyed Poe said. "You are an optimistic man."

"Let us say I have confidence in your talents."

"What makes you think I will not deliberately withhold just to draw the expense money?"

"That is the reason for a progressively declining rate: so there would be less incentive for you to do that very thing. Also, you will be anxious to claim the reward and the fame which accompanies it. But mostly because you are a gentleman, Mr. Poe."

"You are correct, sir. I am a Virginia gentleman, and that will suffice."

"Then the terms are agreed and this contract is in effect on your word?"

"It is indeed," Poe affirmed, with a lightness in his voice Beckwith had not yet heard.

"There is just one more condition before I concur in this agreement," Beckwith added. "That in all instances your statements are to be for my ears only. That you will do exactly what I say at the time I say it. Mr. Poe, we will be embarking on a hazardous expedition, and not all of it involves a homicidal maniac. As I am an appointed official and responsible to an elected one, sometimes decisions are made that will not appeal to your conscience. Nevertheless I must emphasize: Say what you will, protest as you desire, but do nothing but what I ask or you forfeit all."

"You have offered me most generous terms," the author said," and perhaps had you bargained I would have accepted somewhat less. Therefore I accede to this modest codicil. I accept the subordinate position."

"There will be no subordinate or superior stances between us, Mr. Poe," said the Police Superintendent tactfully. "Merely the rendering of mutual assistance. It is my hope that if we do clash it will be as two stones that give off sparks to illuminate."

"Well said, Mr. Beckwith. You are an imaginative and an ambitious man."

"Why do you say that, Mr. Poe?"

"You would not have chosen me to aid you if you were not. It would have been enough to do your job in the routine manner. Yet you would not have it that way. A solution to these murders will bring you high office."

"Perhaps, Mr. Poe. We shall see. If it does, then my investment will have been worth it, will it not? As you are formally in service as an unofficial investigator, can you be at my office at ten o'clock Monday morning? It is in the Old Jail."

"Perhaps you would care to lodge here this evening?" Poe offered.

"I must decline," Beckwith replied. "There are many things requiring my attention even this late. Nor have I made provision for staying elsewhere. However, I must ask a question before I go. Perhaps before 'The Raven' was published you might have been known only to a select audience, but now you are famous. Yet you are impoverished. Have you not gained anything from your works?"

"Yes, from my writings I have gained more of what I already had, ill fortune," said the poet, the intensity of his bitterness rising with each word. "I am here because of pirates. Pirates, sir, that have left me like a derelict in the backwash of this great city. Not pirates like Captain Kidd, whom I wrote about in 'The Gold-Bug.' If Kidd wanted you dead, he ran you through and ended it. These are literary pirates—publishers—committing their crimes brashly and with impunity because there are no enforceable copyright laws. Publishers who take the product of a man's mind, giving him nothing while reaping the fruits of his labor. Who would afford literature as a profession at those wages? Only the dedicated and the inane such as myself."

The author spoke with furious indignation, and Beckwith contrived to disengage from the topic. He wanted Poe in the city. Better to be curt than to impair his timetable.

"It is imperative that I leave now, Mr. Poe. I will see you Monday morning at my office on Chatham Street. Until then, Mr. Poe."

"A good night to you, Mr. Beckwith."

As the Police Superintendent turned, he heard movement on the stairs. Mrs. Clemm was waiting for him when he reached the bottom. He thought that for a large woman she moved quietly.

"Will you have some tea, Mr. Beckwith? It will help to sustain your trip back."

"I am most grateful, ma'am," he replied, "but I am in a hurry."

"Mr. Beckwith, may I be so bold as to ask a question?" she said without diffidence.

"Of course, ma'am."

"Is it correct that you have engaged my son-in-law?" The question was tantamount to an admission of eavesdropping. She is an open woman, thought Beckwith.

"I have retained Mr. Poe to do a service for me."

"Is it possible, then, that I might ask you for an advance? Mr. Poe is too concerned with aesthetics to consider monetary matters, but it is most necessary to make this request. I hope, sir, I am not being too forward."

"Not at all, ma'am. It is a reasonable request. I am the one who should be embarrassed for not suggesting it." He reached into his pockets. "I am sorry, but this is all I have"—indicating the paper and coins he put on a table. It came to about $14. "I hope it is enough for your immediate wants."

"It is more than sufficient, I assure you," Mrs. Clemm said, trying to contain her gladness and restrain her hand from scooping up the pile of money.

"I must go now, ma'am, if I may have my coat. I will not say good-bye to Mrs. Poe for fear of disturbing her. But I am sure I will be returning to renew my acquaintance. Meanwhile, I wish her good health." And Beckwith turned and went through the door held open by Mrs. Clemm.

"Good night, Mr. Beckwith," she called after him, adding quietly, "and God bless you." Her son-in-law was waiting in the kitchen when she returned.

"You should not have been listening at the door, Muddie," Poe said. "I think he knew you were there. I do not mind your hearing anything that passes between myself and others, for you always have my best interest at heart, but it is not in good taste to eavesdrop."

"Nonsense, Eddie dear. Mr. Beckwith did not state his business, but I could not refuse admittance to the Police Superintendent. Still, I would never allow you to be harassed in your own bedroom."

Mrs. Clemm responded casually; she had heard this accusation and the sentiment of gratitude so many times before that she was incapable of making any variation in the reply.

"I hope you did not ask him for money, Muddie. It so detracts from my reputation as a gentleman. I suppose I should be more aggressive, but I just cannot humiliate myself in that manner. Besides, and this is not meant as a chastisement, I cannot help telling you that your acceptance of advances has committed me to projects which have mortified me, undertakings I would have rather starved than lent my good name to. You should consult me before you do these things, Muddie."

Mrs. Clemm flushed but all she said was, "You should be in bed, Eddie dear. You are still not strong enough to be up."

"I must be in the city Monday so I might as well get used to being about."

Poe turned and went through the kitchen door into his writing room, where his wife was in bed. So easily did Virginia become exhausted these days that even at this early hour she was asleep. Already the night sweat had come upon her. Poe gazed at his wife of eleven years. Despite the wasting sickness Virginia still looked as she had at thirteen when he married her. He again imagined the beginning: her always undemanding presence, the lustrous black eyes, and the loving silences.

"You may not be Helen of Troy but you are Penelope of Utica, and she was beautiful too," Poe whispered. He took off the heavy coat he wore and placed it over the blankets. Then he walked rapidly back to the kitchen.

"Ah, Eddie. The soup is almost ready. Do sit and keep me company since you are downstairs. Virginia is probably asleep. I will wake her later. This Beckwith seems like a kind man."

"How kind he is I do not know, but he is generous."

"Generous he is, that's a fact," said Mrs. Clemm.

"Oh, God, Muddie, did you borrow money from him?"

"I only asked for what is your due, Eddie dear," she replied, unperturbed. "I am truly sorry to embarrass you, but if I do not let anyone know our state I cannot get help. They take such advantage of you because you are a gentleman. I too was brought up in a genteel household, in the house of a general. But I am not so fine a lady that it means my tongue should go black with hunger while praising honor's name."

"What you say is true, but what must this Beckwith think of me?"

"Why, what he thought of you before he came through the door of this house. I merely asked for an advance, not for a loan."

"Well, as long as you posed it in that manner. This Beckwith puzzles me. He is so malleable in many respects yet so determined in others. But his being so leaves me a good deal of leeway."

"Eddie, I heard him. What he asked of you was reasonable. He pays you to do exactly what he says. Since he is the law, it gives added weight to his request. I am not the judge of men you are but, as he is both your benefactor and the Police Superintendent, it will not go well should you do other than as he bids."

"No man has a greater will than Edgar Allan Poe. No one will ever tell me what to do. This Beckwith is no exception Muddie, where is it?"

"Where is what?"

"You know what I am referring to."

"You cannot have it, Eddie."

"I need it. Monday will be my first day out. It will be exhausting and I will need sharpened faculties. Where is it?"

"Eddie, please, you can do it. I know you can succeed without it. Things will change and all will be better."

"I want it, Muddie."

Mrs. Clemm knew from the timbre of his voice that it was time to give in. "Very well. Go upstairs, Eddie, and I will bring it to you."

3

DECEMBER 1846

NEW YORK CITY
(Lafayette Place)

Beckwith reached his Lafayette Place residence about an hour after he had left the Poe cottage. Conveniently, there was a stable on Fourth Street so he did not have far to walk to get home. He usually dined out at seven o'clock. If the weather was bad or if he was in the mood for company he went to Vaux Hall Gardens, but routinely he tried the many restaurants downtown. He walked everywhere. He found city life sedentary and so desperately craved exercise that he enrolled in Dr. Rich's Institute for Physical Education, an austere gymnasium on Crosby Street.

Walking had another functional purpose: It enabled him to make sure his men were patrolling properly. His leatherheads—particularly those working at night—now knew that their peripatetic superintendent might appear any time during their shift. Beckwith had fired six men in the first three months of his tenure. He knew his force regarded him as a martinet, and that was exactly the reputation he wanted. Once a policeman he had dismissed for malingering came at him in fury, brandishing his locust stick. He deftly sidestepped the blow, tripped the man, and took the fallen baton. As the man rose to attack again, Beckwith struck him on the side of the head. He then announced that since the man would probably be spending a month in the hospital, that would be his sentence for assaulting a citizen.

Beckwith was cold and tired, but he had no appetite and decided to forego the evening meal. He took off his clothes and let them drop where they were. The cleaning woman would take care of them. He had no housekeeper in the usual sense nor did he want one. He found his world perfect as it was.

His home on Lafayette Place was a find, one of the new types called a New York row house which combined simplicity and grandeur. Stretching along the entire length of the block, the row houses shared a common roof and twenty-eight uniformly spaced, free-standing Corinthian columns. The gates in the wrought-iron fences marked the individual street-level entrances. This level also contained the carriage area and was considered the first floor. A staircase led to the second floor, where there was a hallway which led on the right to the dining room and a kitchen, on the left to a spacious drawing room and, beyond that, a room Beckwith had turned into a library. On the third floor were three large bedrooms, one of which was now a study. This converted room was the situs of his activity, for it was here Beckwith held his interviews and maintained his confidential correspondence with politicians of the Democratic Party and officials of the state and national government.

Beckwith put on his robe and poured himself some whiskey. He walked across the hall, opened the drawer of his writing desk, pulled out a dossier, and sat in an upholstered chair.

The information came from many sources. Beckwith had read the dossier and remembered most of it, but he wanted to refresh himself on certain points. Across the top of the folder in his own small careful printing were the words EDGAR ALLAN POE. He opened it.

1809: Born Edgar Poe in Boston, January 19; mother, stage actress, daughter of English actor parents; father, David

Poe, Jr., of middle-class Baltimore family, who insists on becoming an actor. Mother's second marriage, father's first. Three children reputedly born of union: older son William, Edgar, and daughter, Rosalie. Girl's legitimacy in question since born after father deserts. Father quarrelsome, unstable, a drunkard; aggravated by wife's acting accomplishments while himself only given minor parts, he disappears and his end is unknown.

1811: Mother, Elizabeth Arnold Hopkins Poe, dies in Richmond of consumption. Two-year-old Edgar taken in by Frances and John Allan, he a Scottish-born merchant and storekeeper. Allan does not want the child but takes him at insistence of his beautiful but barren wife.

1815: The Allans sail for England and remain there five years. Young Edgar goes to English schools, excels academically. Takes Allan name but is never adopted. Taunted by schoolmates for being an American and a traitor.

1820: The Allans return to Richmond and Edgar attends several private schools, becoming proficient in classical languages and mathematics.

1824: On his visit to America, the Marquis de Lafayette calls on Grandmother Poe in Baltimore. Edgar's grandfather, David Poe, Sr., had ardently supported the Revolutionary cause to the extent of procuring supplies for the Continental Army from his own purse. This endeared him to Lafayette and the two men became friends. However, the loan was never reimbursed by Congress and from then on the family was always in debt. Young Edgar serves in the honor guard for that august Frenchman in Richmond. With this background, the strangest yet: Because his maternal grandparents had the surname Arnold, Edgar disseminates the story that he is kinsman to Benedict Arnold. That he is related to this infamous traitor, based on the coincidence of his mother's maiden name, is likely a fabrication.

1825: Allan inherits fortune from uncle. Mrs. Allan constantly ill. Allan becomes a heavy drinker, seeks other liaisons. Edgar adopts the airs of the plantation set who spend their summers in townhouses in Richmond, becomes a free-spender with little interest in his foster father's business. Forms strong romantic attachment for a friend's mother, Jane Stith Stanard, who later dies insane.

1826: Poe sent to the University of Virginia. Accumulates large debts trying to maintain the social status of his classmates. Allan refuses to pay. Young Poe discovers that Sarah Elmira Royster, to whom he is informally engaged, is betrothed to another man (probably the result of Allan's declaration that Edgar would not be his heir).

1827: Violent altercations between Poe and foster father. Poe leaves Allan household. Goes to Boston and publishes first poems. Enlists in army. Circulates fabricated stories about himself.

1829: Poe now sergeant-major. Foster mother Frances Allan dies. Poe not informed, finds out later, goes to Richmond. Brief reconciliation with foster father. Buys discharge from army. While awaiting appointment to West Point, stays in household of his aunt, Mrs. Maria Clemm, which includes her daughter, Virginia, then six years old, and Poe's older brother, William, a poet.

1830: At West Point, Poe does well in classwork and in military routines. Beginnings of his bad health.

1831: Poe has himself expelled from West Point. Goes to New York City where his first signed work, *Poems by Edgar A. Poe,* is published, a financial failure. Becomes ill, goes to Mrs. Clemm in Baltimore.

1832: A Philadelphia periodical publishes five of Poe's stories.

1833: He wins first prize of $50 from *Baltimore Saturday Visiter* for his story, "MS. Found in a Bottle." Sells other prose.

1834: John Allan dies, providing for second Mrs. Allan, her children, and his three other bastard offspring by two other women; Poe not mentioned.

1835: Engaged as editor of *Southern Literary Messenger,* Poe brings Mrs. Clemm and Virginia to Richmond. The

33

Messenger becomes one of the nation's leading publications.

1836: Poe marries Virginia Clemm on May 16. She is thirteen years old. Virginia adores her older cousin, and her mother encourages the match.

1837: Poe's talents triple circulation of *Messenger*, enriching owner. Dissatisfied with his meager wages, he moves to New York City.

1838: No employment in New York City. Poe goes to Philadelphia.

1839: Becomes co-editor of *Burton's Gentleman's Magazine*. Publishes *Tales of the Grotesque and Arabesque* and circulates a prospectus for his own magazine. These years the zenith of the poet's prosperity.

1842: Poe joins *Graham's Magazine* and then quits because of low salary. The beginnings of Virginia's continuing illness are diagnosed as consumption. Work tenuous, he decides to return to New York City.

1845: "The Raven" is published. Poe acquires national reputation, becomes part owner of the *Broadway Journal*.

1846: Disputes between Poe and two partners; newspaper goes bankrupt. Unable to afford city rent, Poes move to suburbs.

Summary: Poe is hypersensitive about his age, portrays himself as younger man. He has the reputation of being a lecher. Contrarily, since he has no children, it is bandied about that Poe has never had conjugal relations with his wife, due to his impotence. Yet he has a reputation for lasciviousness. These reports, while incongruous, may be valid since involvement with many women does not necessarily lead to consummation. Also, Poe pronounces spiritual love the highest form of human fulfillment.

Poe is an alcoholic, his nature such that one drink will intoxicate him. His binges aggravate his illnesses and facility for deliriums.

He is an opium eater and a user of morphine.

Poe affects idiosyncratic styles of clothing. In his youth, his raiment was fashioned after his hero, Lord Byron. Now he constantly wears black. It is said he does this to promote the "Raven" image, but he arrayed himself in these funereal clothes long before the poem was published. The somber color of his attire disguises its seediness. The poet owns only two outer garments, a blue-gray guard coat from West Point and a black cloak of the Spanish style.

At this point, Beckwith's eyes became heavy and he set aside the dossier. Poe is indeed enigmatic, bizarrely dichotomized in every aspect, he thought. Born in Boston, he considers himself of the Virginia aristocracy. In many ways a sophisticate, he can also be ingenuous. His writings incisively fathom an unprobed area of the mind, yet he mires himself in an unreal world. He is a poseur yet sensitive of his dignity. Instead of being surfeited of death— his life being full of personal casualties—he is obsessed with the subject.

The contradictions which represented Poe's life seemed interminable, to the extent that Beckwith gave up attempting to enumerate them.

It was early, about ten o'clock. Midnight was the time Beckwith usually retired. Tonight would be the exception, he decided. After checking the pistol on his table, he went to bed.

That night Beckwith had a dream. He was standing in a bleak expanse. His eyes were focused on a huge rectangular form which he made out to be a picture frame. There was a single white dot in the background. As the one-dimensional dot came closer, it became larger and transformed itself into a figure of a man. The man became fixed in the frame as would the subject of a portrait.

The head was surrounded by a mass of black hair, slightly disarranged, as if the frantic effort to comb it had not completely succeeded. The hair had a prominent wave in front and several smaller waves undulating to the back. The midnight hair and eyebrows, the haughty moustache, all contrasted with the colorless flesh of the face. The mesmeric eyes were staring, fixed on some indefinable point beyond. The nose was longish, the right nostril larger than the left, destroying the symmetry of the handsome features. There was a smile on the thin pursed lips. The black jacket was open, revealing a black-and-white striped shirt and a cream cravat, loosely tied. The portrait was Poe.

(In Beckwith's dream he was not at all surprised it was Poe, as if he had had advance intelligence that the poet would be the subject of his dream.)

Poe's lips and mouth became mercurial as a variety of smiles followed each other in rapid succession: whimsical, sly, quixotic, enigmatic, soulful, rueful, seraphic, haunting, cherubic, demonic, beatific, malevolent, benevolent. Then the figure of the poet split —first into two parts, next into four, then into eight—a vertiginous shattering, but of a precise geometric progression. Then a decrescendo, ending with a reticulation of white dots, representing a galaxy of Poes.

Beckwith then saw side by side a witches' coven and an assemblage of the heavenly host. Below the pointed hats and the halos, all the figures had the face of Poe.

And so it was with all things appearing within the frame: with the creatures of the earth and the sky, of the sea and under the sea, whether living or imagined—all bore Poe's visage.

Then another brisance: Poe as the figurehead of a sailing ship, as the tip of a lightning rod, superimposed on pieces of famous sculptures. Poe as the sphinx, the Medusa, a unicorn, a phoenix, a gargoyle. And so into the frame came a cascading torrent of images. Again, the portrait of Poe as he appeared initially: the mournful smile, the searching eyes.

Beckwith awoke because of a severe cramp in his right leg. He was annoyed, not at the dream or at the awakening but at the pain in his leg. He thought of himself as a perfect physical specimen. His one flaw was this cramp in his leg which could come to him unpredictably. There was no telling when the calf muscles would tighten and there would be excruciating pain for a time. This concern for his one physical imperfection stayed with him until he again fell asleep.

4

DECEMBER 1846

NEW YORK CITY
(Chatham Street)

"Good morning, Mr. Poe. You are prompt. It is exactly ten o'clock. Do sit down and let us get to it."

Poe looked no different from Beckwith's dream the previous night. He carried his wool guard coat and hat and wore his usual black attire. The only thing added was a walking stick with the three-headed Cerberus as its top.

The poet surveyed the room. The double windows faced out on Chatham Street. The walls, evidently of the same thick stone material as the cells on the other floors, had a fresh coat of green paint over many other layers of paint. There were no decorations except for uniform framed illustrations of the Presidents of the United States in order of their assumption of office. Poe's amused reaction to the display was that for an ardent Democrat, Beckwith was surprisingly bipartisan. Directly in front of the windows was the Police Superintendent's wooden desk. To the right of the desk, in the corner, was a three-stanchioned flag holder looking like an oversized candelabrum; the lower held the flags of the City of New York and New York State, the upper the American flag. On the wall was a huge map of the municipality with indications of ward and legislative boundaries, fire districts, hydrants, public cisterns, wharves, and a listing of buildings including churches, hotels, and markets. On another table was a pile of city directories going back over the years and a stack of maps.

"Before I begin, Mr. Poe, I must ask you not to make any notes. Everything is to be committed to memory. The details of these crimes have not been released. As you may be aware, when such a crime is committed there are disturbed persons who come forth to confess. By withholding some of the facts, it is possible to determine if one of these persons is actually the murderer. It is these details which I now relate.

"On the fourth of September, at approximately ten fifty P.M., the body of a young woman was discovered on Rivington Street about three blocks from the East River wharves. It was found by an Edward Penny, a volunteer fireman from Live Oak Engine Number Forty-four, which has its firehouse on Houston Street, two blocks north. At first, he thought the body was that of a prostitute who had had too much to drink. These women frequent that area to solicit the sailors from the ships docked there or the stevedores who patronize the many taverns in the area. As Penny approached the form, so horrid was the spectacle it almost petrified him. It was a girl. Her skirt had been pulled up and there was no underclothing. I do not mean that it was just ripped or torn away, but every article below the waist, except for the skirt, was stripped off. There was not a shred of her underclothes— except for the strip around her throat. This young woman was subsequently identified as Angelina Van Cortlandt.

"Examination of the body revealed stab wounds just above the vaginal area in and around the pubic hair. These wounds, it seems, were made with a small sharp instrument, perhaps a pocketknife. The wounds were superficial but multiple, as if the wielder had plunged the weapon into her body in a frenzy. However, they were not meant to kill her. She was already dead—how long, our medical examiner could not be sure, perhaps minutes, perhaps a half hour. This was ascertained because the blood did not readily flow.

"The cause of death was strangulation. A piece of petticoat

was tied around her neck and then twisted to squeeze the breath out of her. It was done with just enough strength to stop her breathing; it did not break the skin. This was determined by the depth of the red mark encircling her throat. There also was a bluish tinge to the skin, for what is garroting but asphyxiation? Also, there was a slight swelling of her face and foam about the mouth. From this, it was concluded that she was throttled just sufficiently to kill her or render her unconscious—"

"It is quite possible that she was alive when the stab wounds were inflicted," Poe interrupted.

"Yes, though this cannot positively be stated," Beckwith replied. "Legal medicine being what it is today, we cannot be sure of the sequence."

"Whoever did this was a ghoul," said the poet.

"I am not quite finished, Mr. Poe. There are more peculiarities to relate. Mixed with the blood in the vaginal area was semen."

"You mean she was violated after she was dead?" Poe asked.

"If violated is the euphemism for sexual intercourse, the answer is yes."

"How horrible!" the writer said.

"I have not yet completed the account," Beckwith declaimed. "Above the girl's head, written in her own blood, was the number thirteen."

"Thirteen, you say?"

"Apparently. These blood numerals were written by someone wearing black gloves of the common sort, purchasable in any emporium or men's furnishing store."

"But you said your men were unable to find a trace of abandoned clothing in the area."

"Correct. There was no need to search for the gloves. They were neatly laid beside the body. And from them we can perhaps progress to two more indications: the size of the murderer and that he was right-handed."

"I know how you are able to tell he was right-handed," the

39

poet said. "There would be blood on the index finger of the right glove."

"Precisely, Mr. Poe. As to his size, you too will be able to tell that, I am sure, when you see the gloves. It was this pair." Beckwith opened a drawer and laid the gloves on the desk within reach of the poet. "You see, Mr. Poe, the gloves fit me. This should indicate a man about my size wore them. Let us say someone about one hundred eighty pounds and six feet tall."

"But whoever used the gloves," Poe surmised as he examined them, "shaped the index finger out of proportion by pressing down heavily when he wrote the numerals. See, the finger is much wrinkled because there was no digit to fill it. This is indicated by blood in the creases farther down the finger than the tip, proving the finger did not fill out to its full size. My conclusion is that in leaving the gloves the killer was deliberately trying to make you think he was a larger man."

"Precisely, Mr. Poe. It was just a flourish on the Garroter's part—a sort of invitation to a challenge. Else, being so careful in everything, why leave the gloves? Or, for that matter, the other indicator, the bloody thirteen?"

"Then your killer would have to be smaller than six feet tall and less than one hundred and eighty pounds," Poe hypothesized.

"I would say someone about your size and weight," Beckwith agreed. "We will also have to conclude that the person we are seeking may be not only insane but ingenious. Every aspect of these murders was carefully executed. Nothing appears spontaneous. Foremost, let us consider the location and then the crimes.

"The body of Miss Van Cortlandt was found in an area which, while not as heavily trafficked as a main thoroughfare, is near warehouses which are patrolled by watchmen and the police. Then there are the sailors who come and go from their ships and patronize the nearby taverns. Our murderer invited attention by coming into this particular street. And he took further chances.

"Miss Van Cortlandt's body was positioned in the middle of the block. Certainly the killer's chance of discovery would have been lessened had he chosen a more secluded street to dispose of her body. No, the murderer picked his location purposefully. Consider his fastidiousness: the arranged position of the body, skirt neatly pulled up, every fold in place; the thirteen which had been written in her blood; her underclothes neatly shorn away from the waist down. Perhaps he even took the time to ejaculate there; that is a possibility too."

"Indecent, positively indecent," Poe remonstrated.

"Do you mean the murder or the way she was found?" Beckwith flashed. "Because if you mean that she was nude from the waist down, I am sure that a sense of propriety was of no comfort to Miss Van Cortlandt at the time. And if we are going to deal with these matters, Mr. Poe, we must not be inhibited by the prudery of language. That can be reserved for the literary magazines and not for this investigation. At least it will not be on my part. However, I am perfectly willing to accept your semantic limitations and sensibilities just so we are sure as to exact meanings."

The poet flushed, was about to reply, but restrained himself.

Beckwith continued. "If how Miss Van Cortlandt was brought to the scene of her final disposition was clever, let us then consider what happened prior to that event.

"Killing the girl was the easiest part. I am sorry to plunge ahead of you here, Mr. Poe, but I have reviewed these facts many times and have already mulled over several corollaries. Miss Van Cortlandt had to be maneuvered into being his victim. Whom was he dealing with? She was not an ordinary girl. She was as close to aristocracy as it is possible to become in this New World, a descendent of Dutch patroons who had settled here before the Duke of York conquered New Amsterdam. Therefore, Miss Cortlandt is hardly the type of girl who would be permitted out unescorted."

The writer broke in. "Your point is that whoever murdered her knew full well the victim he wanted?"

"Precisely, Mr. Poe. Miss Cortlandt was not a random victim. There is an almost decorous element involved here. She either had to be cleverly deceived or she knew the person who enticed her to her death."

"And have you traced her movements for that day?"

"I have," Beckwith responded. "Miss Van Cortlandt was attending a literary soiree in the home of Alicia Schuyler, the second victim. We have a list of people attending."

"And they are?"

"I will get to that in a moment, for it is pertinent in forming the relationship between the two murders. However, I think it will profit us more to examine the second murder.

"Three days ago, on December fourth, at four ten in the afternoon, Alicia Schuyler left her home near St. John's Park. Miss Schuyler did not have the permission of her parents to leave her residence. But as you have noted, Mr. Poe, Alicia was an audacious young lady, who hardly could be tethered. She was seen by a servant slipping out the front door. Exactly why she left is unknown. However, it is thought that she went to meet a young man who had been paying court to her. We have several witnesses who identified her leaving the opposite end of the park on Varick Street. This was about four twenty P.M. It being a dreary day, darkness came early. That was the last time the ebullient Miss Schuyler was seen alive.

"At about eleven fifteen that evening, on Delancey Street, between Columbia and Cannon streets, less than one-half mile from where Angelina Van Cortlandt was found, a laborer named James Lewis, who had just come from one of the taverns, saw the body of a young girl lying on the ground. He immediately sounded the alarm. It was the dead Miss Schuyler and she had been, as had been Miss Van Cortlandt, brutally strangled. In fact, except for the location, the crime was almost a replication of the first murder.

"Miss Schuyler was found with a strip from her petticoat around her throat. Her skirt was pulled over her torso, with every fold in place. There was no trace of her underclothing, although nothing had been torn away. From the waist down, her body was exposed."

"And, I suppose," Poe broke in, "that there was semen in the vaginal area and that she had been repeatedly stabbed there."

"Quite correct," Beckwith affirmed. "And the number thirteen was found written in her blood, with the same type of gloves lying at her side. However, there was an added detail."

"And that was?" the poet asked.

"When my man bent to examine Miss Schuyler, he smelled the distinct odor of ether."

"Then we now know," the author declared, "how the murderer was able to render his victims inert."

"Also that he killed her not too long before he disposed of her," Beckwith added. "Had she been in the street for any time the ether would have evaporated. We can now surmise the time for the killer to dispatch his victim. Miss Schuyler was last seen at about four thirty P.M. and her body was found past ten o'clock. That gave our murderer less than six hours to proceed through each phase of his plan."

"That he used ether will do you little good," Poe said. "It is a common item sold at any druggist's shop. In fact, it is the fashion these days for literary ladies to douse their handkerchiefs with ether to help sustain themselves against a callous world."

"I suppose it is no more silly than men using snuff; however, ether is a most dangerous chemical to be toying with. There are experimentations going on with it at Columbia Medical College. It will be used as an anesthetic in a surgical operation soon. Knowing about these women's affectations makes me grateful."

"For what?"

"That I am not acquainted with any of your literary ladies," Beckwith retorted. "Nevertheless, I had my men check all the chemist's shops in the city. As you anticipated, nothing came of it."

All this time the Police Superintendent had been walking about the room. His action was that of a frenetic professor who has just finished a crucial part of his lecture. He then sat down in the chair, but after a momentary pause he was up on his feet again, pacing as he resumed his recounting.

"Mr. Poe, I will now recapitulate these crimes. I would appreciate your comments on any aspect, any detail which has eluded me, any point which would illuminate—no matter how inconsequential it seems or how outrageously it defies logic. Also, Mr. Poe, we will be spending a good deal of time together. I think it will be easier if we dropped the *Mr.* when addressing each other. So if you have no objections I will call you by your surname and you may call me by mine. You have no objections, do you, Poe?"

"Certainly not, *Mr.* Beckwith," the poet responded. There was a moment of silence and then they both laughed.

"Now, Poe, we will itemize the details of the crimes. The victims are both young girls about seventeen years old, both viciously abused, both of aristocratic families which date to before the Revolution. Angelina Van Cortlandt and Alicia Schuyler were not only friends but had the same interest—literature. However, the girls were of different physical characteristics, in stature and in coloring. So we can disregard the premise that the victims were ideal models the Garroter may have wished to revenge himself on. That is all I can mark in this category."

"Are you not forgetting another singular element, Beckwith? Both crimes were committed on the fourth day of the month. Could that be a coincidence?"

"No, the dates do not escape me, Poe. Perhaps it could have meaning. Our killer could be in an occupation or on a travel route at this time of the month which makes it possible for him to pursue his purpose."

"Or it could be that to the Garroter this number, as in the thirteen scrawled about the victim's head, has some supernatural significance," said Poe.

"That may well be," Beckwith replied. "However, I do not lean in that direction. In ritualistic murder, the tendency is to select random victims. I think we can dismiss this possibility unless some other piece of evidence comes forth.

"The question is whether the Van Cortlandts and the Schuylers had any other relationship: some common enemy wishing vindication for a real or fancied wrong. I come up blank here, Poe. The Van Cortlandts do not involve themselves directly in politics, and their income derives from their huge tracts of land. The family is now selling most of its holdings in lower Manhattan; the rest of their land is leased to tenant farmers in the Pelham area. And, except for an occasional prudent investment in ships' cargoes and maritime insurance, the Van Cortlandts are not involved in any commercial enterprises. The Schuylers' erstwhile scion, Alexander Hamilton, was deeply involved in politics, which has a propensity for making mortal enemies. However, as Hamilton's son, Peter, left the faith of his father, the Federalist Party, the Schuylers have also withdrawn from politics. This I can personally attest to, as an observer of that scene. There is only one bond between the two families, their daughters.

"Angelina Van Cortlandt and Alicia Schuyler shared an interest in literature. Note that Miss Van Cortlandt was abducted after a soiree in her friend's home. Miss Schuyler was taken the afternoon of a scheduled literary function at her home. But you should know this. You attended the first and received an invitation to the second."

"I—I certainly did not," the author stammered uncharacteristically. "I did receive an invitation from Miss Van Cortlandt for September fourth, but as I was completing 'The Cask of Amontillado' I did not attend. I know nothing about Miss Schuyler's invitation. But that is not unusual. There is no post office at Fordham village; the closest one is at West Farms, two miles away. I have not had a chance to get there these past three weeks, having been incapacitated. I still have not been there."

"Evidently, my information is incorrect, Poe. It is immaterial. I was merely wondering why you did not mention it. Let us proceed. As we examine this facet of the two girls' activities, the thread is literature. It seems there is a group, including both girls, which meets often and attends the same events. Are you aware of the particular following that I am referring to?"

"Now that you mention it, on several instances I did note that the same young ladies were together. There was Angelina Van Cortlandt, Alicia Schuyler, Joan Jay, Sarah Lewissohn, and Priscilla Livingston. There were others, but these were a constellation. In fact, these young ladies used to refer to themselves frivolously as the Literary Liaison. They had nothing more serious in mind than a reading of poetry. Their profound discussions concerned which suitors their parents might approve."

"And this was all that any of these girls discussed in detail?"

"Beckwith, you must remember that in social status I am worthy to be in their circle, but I am penniless. I had little contact with these young ladies or their group except when invited to their literary teas to read for a fee. What I know about them was gleaned from overheard conversations and social items in the press."

"Poe, you are an asset. You have confirmed some preliminary information. From my reports, besides the two murdered girls, I have established, by comparing the list of attendees, the presence of five others who were to be at both literary affairs. Perhaps it is a coincidence, but it is just as good a starting point as any."

"And these five are?"

Beckwith opened the drawer and pulled out a dossier. He took the contents and placed it on the desk at the farthest point from where Poe was sitting. But the author had been in the composing room of many publications and had acquired the type-setter's trick of reading print not only backward but upside down. So despite Beckwith's maneuver Poe noted that written in small, careful print across the top was LITERARY LIAISON GROUPING. I apparently told him nothing he did not know before, Poe thought. I have added negligibly to what he could have deduced himself. In many ways, I am a hindrance to him. Why does he want me?

"Poe, here are the candidates. Our first profile concerns John Moran, a man with many prominent connections. He is a vice-president of the Bank of Manhattan on Beaver Street and was a member of the board of directors of the Bank of the United States before President Jackson dissolved it. Moran was reputed to be a backer of Aaron Burr, who founded the Bank of Manhattan and whose aborted attempt to dismember the United States by plotting to seize our western territories resulted in his trial for treason. Moran is thirty-nine years old and a bachelor. He lived with his mother until she died two years ago. He was devoted to her, and after her death he closed his house on MacDougal Street and left the country for two years on a grand tour of Europe. Moran does no entertaining, and admission to his home is difficult. It is reported that there is no portrait of a woman or female form in his entire house. He is a total abstainer but does favor Havana cigars, which, by the way, Poe, he purchases daily at John Anderson's Tobacco Shop, where Mary Rogers was working when she was murdered. His vocation is making money, his avocation is civic betterment, and his sole pleasure apparently is supporting theatrical and literary projects. He attends all performances at the Park Row Theater and Castle Garden. On these occasions he attends alone or with a party such as the Literary Liaison. He has never been accompanied by a woman—"

"As a sponsor of these theatrical events," Poe interrupted, "he must be acquainted with many of the actresses. Is he known to request their favors?"

"Poe, your euphemisms can be delicate. If you are asking if he sleeps with the actresses, I have no answer. My material is cursory simply because there was never a need officially for any data on him. Besides, Moran shuns notice. This would be natural after the Burr escapade, because for a time it seemed that the Bank of Manhattan would be destroyed by that association. Now he does not align himself publicly with any political faction, though I know that he surreptitiously contributes to both the Whig and Native American parties.

47

"Our next profile concerns Count Paul Gilbert Motier of Montpellier. He has many more intermediary Christian names, but the two should suffice. This Frenchman claims to be the nephew of the Marquis de Lafayette. He is about twenty-four and handsome. He came to this country two years ago, but otherwise nothing is known about him. I have checked with my sources at the French consulate in the city, but they could not enlighten me further. He appears to be penniless. He is living in a boarding-house on Rector Street. However, he dresses quite well, attends all the social functions, and though he is tardy in payment of his bills he manages to keep his creditors satisfied. However, periodically he absents himself from the city for two to three days, and when he returns he pays all his debts. He makes no particular secret of his impecuniousness, since his noble birth erases all deficiencies of character and intelligence he might possess."

"Spoken like a true republican," Poe commented, not bothering to disguise the sardonic double entendre. Having been heckled at rowdy political rallies, Beckwith ignored the twitting.

"Count Motier's objective is plain enough: to marry money. For as soon as he arrived from France and settled in the city he insinuated himself into the upper social circles and courted Alicia Schuyler, Joan Jay, and Priscilla Livingston alternately. His dash is evidently greater than his strategy. He is obvious. The families recognize him as a fortune hunter, but with his noble background and the reputation of his uncle they tolerate him. The girls cannot take him seriously but nevertheless adore him, particularly the unfortunate Alicia Schuyler."

"And undoubtedly Motier is the one who it is suspected that Miss Schuyler left her home to meet the day of her murder," Poe ventured. "Why, if he flits in that fashion, did he not make the complete circuit and give his attentions as well to Angelina Van Cortlandt and Sarah Lewissohn?"

"Because for the Van Cortlandts, even the kin of Lafayette is not pure enough for mating," Beckwith replied. "The Dauphin, if he appears, would not do because he is Catholic. The family only considers eligible a male of Dutch ancestry and of their Reformed Church. This religious exclusivity applies to Sarah Lewissohn as well. She is of the Hebrew faith, and her family would block any attempt at matrimony outside the religion, even if the young girl loved the Count."

The poet was inwardly furious as he heard this, for it exhumed memories of his love affair with Sarah Elmira Royster of Richmond. They had made vows to each other in her garden the day before he went off to the University of Virginia. She subsequently was forced into marrying another man. This all resulted because his foster father broadcast to Richmond society that Poe was not to be his heir.

"If it is so blatant that this Count Motier is a scoundrel—for that is what he is to me—why is he countenanced in Knickerbocker society?"

"Ah, Poe, that is easy to answer," Beckwith said, aware of the poet's hurtful experience in Richmond and therefore trying to be soft in his reply. "Our country is young. This year will mark the seventh decade of our independence. But in our free-enterprise society we have already formed traditions. It seems that there are three methods of making a success in America: The first is to make a fortune through hard work, the second is to be a speculator, and the third is to marry money. The prime example of marrying wealth is, of course, Alexander Hamilton, who came here from his native West Indies at seventeen. He was not only penniless but of illegitimate birth. However, he was also brilliant in every aspect, and he proved it beyond doubt by wedding General Schuyler's daughter. Seriously though, Poe, I do need your assistance with the Count. You speak French. You also met Lafayette. Talk to Motier. Ask him intimate details about his uncle and the region he claims to be from. Tell me if this Count Motier is a counterfeit."

"I will do my best," said Poe.

"Next in our profile is Philip Lewissohn, Sarah's cousin, an importer of fine diamonds and gems. Philip is twenty-four and an excellent pianist. In fact he has a passion for it and practices incessantly. Odd, for a man of commerce. He is a native of Berlin, where his branch of the family originated. Solomon Lewissohn, his uncle and Sarah's father, came from Frankfurt-am-Main after the American Revolution. Both the young man's parents were killed in a steamer accident on the Rhine. He survived the ship's explosion and was in a hospital for a long period afterward. When he recuperated he was sent for. Sarah Lewissohn is an only child. It is expected that she will be heir to the family fortune and he to the family business."

"You say 'expected to be given' with a hint of doubt," noted Poe.

"There is a conflict between the young man and his benefactors," Beckwith said. "You see, Philip is in love with Priscilla Livingston, and the Lewissohns are Orthodox Jews. The same restrictions which apply to their daughter, Sarah, also prohibit Philip from marrying outside his faith."

"And does Priscilla Livingston return his affection?"

"From my reports, she does. In fact, they are rumored to be lovers."

"If Priscilla is enamored of the young man then there are problems," the poet said.

"More so than appears on the surface. Philip is not only opposed by his kin but, as expected, by the Livingston clan as well. They are of Anglo-Dutch origins and the acme of society. But then the Lewissohns are not exactly recent arrivals in this country either. Nevertheless, Philip faces formidable opposition from both families, although his most desperate opposition is from Priscilla."

"I thought you said the girl loves him."

"She does, and would give—or has given—herself to him. But being a Livingston she is her father's daughter and would not disobey his wishes. She will marry whomever he designates. That is why Priscilla is given rein."

"This Philip Lewissohn must be an extremely frustrated

young man," Poe said, reminiscences of his Richmond days again bounding into his consciousness.

"That there is positive proof of," Beckwith recounted. "About a year ago, to end this affair, Philip Lewissohn decided to visit relatives in Berlin. He spent about thirteen months leisurely getting to his destination. If Philip hoped the trip would be Lethean he must have been bitterly disappointed. For when he returned he was as hopelessly in love with Priscilla as he was when he left, at least that is the appearance."

"And you do not trust appearances of lovers—or anyone else," Poe said.

"Particularly of lovers and generally of anyone else," was Beckwith's rejoinder. "Philip's situation brought him another antagonism."

"No doubt with the Count Motier, whose amorous meanderings took him into the wake of Priscilla Livingston," Poe surmised.

"Precisely, Poe. There were blows and intentions of a duel. Motier undoubtedly would have killed him."

"And what was the result?"

"The Count apologized to Philip—that is, without appearing to detract from his honor—and tacitly agreed to keep his distance from Miss Livingston."

"It was a chivalrous gesture on his part, worthy of a nephew of Lafayette."

"How romantic you are, Poe. It happened to be the most judicious thing to do. Suppose the Count insisted on the duel. He probably would have killed young Lewissohn. The upshot of that would have been social ostracism, irrevocably separating him from any of the girls inclined to marry him. Motier's action shows either that he has excellent advisers or that he is a wily young rascal. Whether he is worse remains to be seen.

"Our last profiles, Poe, are coupled and include the British envoy-general, Sir Richard Townshend, and his wife, Madelyn."

To Poe—whose inbred sense of Southern cavalier was supplemented by his ideal of woman as the poetic embodiment of beauty—it was inconceivable that a female be considered as a suspect. At the mention of the diplomat's wife, Poe could not mask his ire. "Surely, Beckwith, you are not going to include a woman on your list. This is not only offensive to gentlemen, it is patently illogical. Two things dismiss such a proposition as absurd: the garroting of the victims and the semen."

Beckwith responded in a tone which was to the poet disconcertingly unemotional. "Logic, like truth, can go in several directions, depending on which way it is cast. Facts are immutable, truth is not. Facts are ingredients; stirred in different ways, they give different recipes. A fact rearranged is a truth altered.

"I will tell you something, Poe. I expect the Garroter to kill again. I cannot afford to discount any possibility, no matter how outlandish or how much it offends anyone's sense of social convention to accuse a woman of murder. After all, who should know more about bizarre situations than you, who had an orangutan commit two hideous killings in 'The Murders in the Rue Morgue'?

"Let us examine the feminine aspect, since you introduced the subject. First, you did not let me complete my recounting. Had you done so, I would have considered your gentlemanly stance with more regard. However, to the substantive matters that you brought up, the garroting and the semen.

"If you recall my description of the garroting, you will remember that the mark around the throats of both girls was barely visible. This indicates that once that strip of petticoat was affixed only minimal pressure was applied. Why? Was their conscious suffering an integral part of the murderer's satisfaction? Or does it indicate some handicap such as fragility on the part of the killer? And what is fragility associated with? With women, as you have written so often, Poe.

"Also, undoubtedly this is the work of a deranged person. An uncategorized madness, to be sure, but still madness. It is a fact that frenzied people, through some physiological phenomenon, are endowed with enormous strength. Can we exempt a woman? "Then there is the element of entrapment. The killer had to get his victim to a destined place. These young ladies would not have gone with just anyone. It had to be someone they were acquainted with or at least did not suspect. Who could better make such a deception, who would be less susceptible to suspicion by a young girl, than another woman?"

The writer put up his arm in protest and was about to speak, but was not allowed to.

"Ah, Poe, forgive me if I do not allow your presentment at this moment. I feel the great pressure of time. I was hoping that we would be further advanced, for I have something scheduled for this afternoon. I wish you to be completely informed by that time. I anticipate your protest. You are going to say, Well, that is all very logical though it goes against my grain . . ."

"It goes against my grain," the poet got out.

". . . but what about the semen? Every argument for making a woman a candidate for the murderer is nullified by the presence of the semen. Poe, again forgive me if what I say unintentionally offends you, but you have led a sheltered life vis-à-vis what I have seen of depravity in this city. So believe me when I say that it would be easy for a woman to obtain semen at short notice. There are several ways, but let me suggest just one to demonstrate the point. Remember, the victims were found close to populated areas where there was traffic about. With the victim inert or dead, a woman merely need approach any man on the street and offer to place her hand inside his trousers. How many men, particularly in that neighborhood, would have refused? Imagine the response if she offered to pay. So I cannot dismiss the notion that the Garroter may be a woman.

"Which brings me to the profile of Madelyn Townshend. You understand, Poe, that since Sir Richard and his wife are foreigners, as is the Count Motier, my apparatus for collating information about them is not as effective as with the others. One simply does not go to the English consulate and ask for their biography. So despite my contacts here and in the Federal City there is a paucity of information about this couple. Their background perhaps will explain why.

"Lady Townshend is about twenty-eight. She is the daughter of a minor career official in the British foreign service, recently retired, who served most of his years abroad. She is learned, well read, and proficient in languages. Her mother died early. She is an only child. Here is the part that should interest us. Her father seems to have educated her as if she were his son. She is a vigorous sportswoman, participating in all physical types of activities, including fox hunting and fencing. When riding she insists on mounting a horse like a man. Her physique is capable of bearing these strenuous exercises. She is five feet, six inches tall and obviously attractive. Listen to this part, Poe. My investigator is positively rapturous: *'She is well made in every proportion and lithe in her movements. She is Venus adorned.'* My agent seems to have lost his perspective. One could almost discern him wishing to record, *She is Venus unadorned.*

"After her father's retirement in London about three years ago, the lady became part of the retinue of Queen Victoria. She was evidently favored. However, it seems that pressure was brought upon her to marry Sir Richard. It was said to be not her desire but ordered by the Queen herself. That benevolent monarch thought she was aiding Madelyn, since the lady was still unwed, with no dowry and no prospects. By marrying her to a titled gentlemen, minor though he turns out to be, Victoria probably thought she was assuring the security of one of her favored ladies, which was exactly what that strong-willed Queen accomplished.

"Evidently Lady Townshend did not feel any sort of gratitude to Her Majesty for this royally arranged wedding. She expressed her sentiment in a way Victoria would understand without directly insulting that most imperial monarch. It seems that soon after her marriage there were stories of indiscretions. I cannot know if this was true in England, but the lady seems to have her dalliances here. Her husband is often away and there are reports of trysts. There is one particular man who has been often at the envoy-general's home in Greenwich Street during the night hours when it was known that Sir Richard was out of the city. His identity has not been established. This man seems to favor the color gray. He is always seen in the same attire, gray suit, gray gloves, and gray cloak. She is also linked to Harrison Carpentar, who dogs her when her husband is out of the city. He is an enormously attractive lout, Poe, though he has the brains of a poodle. In this comparison between the two, it is the man who suffers. Carpentar is probably the sort who would suit a debauched English noblewoman."

"I know that you will think me hopelessly ingenuous," Poe countered, happy of the opportunity to make a point and to let Beckwith know he was not cowed. (It was not often he allowed another to dominate a conversation.) "You are now doing what you chastise me for, judging on the basis of assumptions. You yourself said there is no corroboration that these reported meetings are assignations. By your own words, you cannot be sure of the stories from England and you cannot establish the identity of her nocturnal visitor. Would it not be better for her reputation to have this obnoxious Carpentar give chase in the open than letting it not be known at all? Your chauvinism is apparent from the phrase 'debauched English noblewoman.' "

"Ah, Poe, you are a romantic, but I will concede. Let us then say *allege* and *seems* and *evidently* until I have warrant to make unqualified statements. For you led me to the next point. Why Lady Townshend is allegedly unfaithful is not evident in my profile of Sir Richard.

"My preliminary report tells nothing of the origins of Richard Townshend. It is said that he became a gentleman farmer in the Westmorland district after a long army career. He was unknown to the royal court until about two years ago, when his name was on the Queen's birthday list for a knighthood. His title is a gesture of honor, what is called a noninheritable baronetcy, the lowest order of peerage. This belated award was given to him for valor during the Second War with England. What specific action merited this recognition is unmentioned. It seems the records were lost, and that is why there was no official acknowledgment at an earlier date. Does this raise an interesting calculation for your assiduous mathematical mind, Poe?"

"Yes," replied the poet. "If he fought in the War of 1812, even just the latter part, it would make Townshend about fifty years old."

"Precisely, Poe. He is in his late forties or early fifties. But be not deceived by his age. I myself have not seen him, but I understand him to be quite the swashbuckler, like someone out of Scott. Straight as a ramrod, courtly in manner, in excellent health, and skillful with a pistol and sword. A man half his age would put him down at peril of life. It is said that just while in London he killed three men in duels, two by pistol, one by the sword. His background could well be authentic. However, I do not trust the entire account, for with enough money, any honor is purchasable in the commercial English court. On the other hand, the story is so ridiculous as to be true. And why not, Poe? In those days, boys started out soldiering at a young age. How old were the members of the Corps of Cadets when you were at West Point in 1830?"

"They were mostly sixteen and seventeen years old, but I know that before my tour there were cadets at ages fourteen and fifteen," Poe said softly, again startled into revealing another painful experience, one he had been attempting to eradicate by giving out that he had been touring Europe during those years.

"And should the present war with Mexico go badly," the Police Superintendent said, "I would imagine that the cadets would be pressed into service. So it is possible to accept that Townshend began his military career quite young. However, it is his present age which concerns us most. The profile states that he looks no older than forty, that he and his wife often ride and are otherwise seen together. There is no surface estrangement. So it would seem that a physical mismatch is not the source of her marital discontentment. Of course, there is the point made about his wife's previous conduct. Townshend may have received his post as a punishment, not a reward. You may be aware, Poe, that the English consider assignment to Washington as onerous. Compared to any of the capitals of Europe, our Federal City is a desolate pesthole, particularly in the summer. Having been there many times I sadly tend to agree. Still, Sir Richard was appointed envoy-general representing the most powerful nation in the world in our city. His only superior is Great Britain's ambassador to the United States. Well, Poe, that ends my listing."

As he concluded, Beckwith gathered up the individual profiles he had tossed on his desk. Placing them in the folder, he put the package in his desk drawer.

"Will I be given the opportunity to review the dossier?"

"Most certainly, Poe. It will be available to you at my home this evening. First, I must delete any matter which reveals the identity of my informants. Everything else will be intact."

"And what happens now?"

"Why, now," said Beckwith, reaching into his inside jacket pocket and pulling out his watch, "it is time for lunch."

"Is that the important engagement you mentioned?" responded Poe.

They looked at each other a moment and then they both laughed.

5

DECEMBER 1846

NEW YORK CITY
(Coffee House Slip)

Poe and Beckwith came out of the Old Jail into the glare of high noon. For the first time in four days there was no chilling wind. The City Hall Park fountain was on, and the jets in the center formed a tiara of glistening sunlight. Multitudes of promenaders and street hawkers mingled with clerks and laborers along the tree-lined Broadway. Horse-drawn cabs, dray carts, and delivery wagons added to the glut of private and hired carriages competing for space on the wide cobblestoned thoroughfare. Nowhere were there signs that the nation was at war.

The poet, anticipating his first substantial midday meal in about a month, swung his walking stick jauntily. He kept in step despite the longer stride of the taller Police Superintendent.

"Is there any place you prefer to eat?" Beckwith politely inquired.

"I leave the choice to you," Poe replied.

"I always have something plain for the noon meal, nor do I have any spirits at this time of day. I trust that is satisfactory," Beckwith said, offering a pronouncement rather than a choice. He had no intention of exposing Poe to alcoholic beverages. Tonight would be a crucial test, and he wanted the poet to have a clear head. "We will go to Coffee House Slip and from there make our choice. You do not mind the walk, do you? It is only seven blocks."

"Walking is about the only exercise I get," Poe said. "Sometimes it is a mandatory one. Many a time I have not had the fare to get back to Fordham and have had to return by foot. At those times I would think of my days with the First Artillery Battalion and pretend I was on a forced march."

"Then your illness does not affect you physically?" Beckwith asked.

"Fortunately, no," replied the poet.

Then, pausing a moment, Poe asked himself in which manner was he fortunate. His horrific sessions of delirium tremens, his beguiling hallucinogenic states, or his fitful periods of brain fevers had the same result—prolonged disability. Which was better, to be incapacitated by a mental disorientation or an organic impairment? It was like asking an artist which he preferred, to be blind or have his painting arm amputated.

"Yes, either way it is a great pity," Beckwith declaimed.

These words so shook Poe that he nearly dropped his cane. In the sunshine, bright but lacking any warmth, in the crowded streets of the port city, a terrifying sense of *déjà vu* came upon him.

How can he know what I am thinking? I am the one who is supposed to be the acute deducer. Has Beckwith the ability to divine my thoughts as my fictive Dupin was able to do to his companion in a similar scene of two characters walking on a Paris street in "The Murders in the Rue Morgue"?

The real pair had walked two blocks on Nassau Street and had just turned left onto Maiden Lane. I am corporeal, Poe protested, and swore he would go mad if the Police Superintendent turned to him to explain the sequence of events which revealed his exact thoughts at that moment as he had Dupin do in that story.

It was with relief he heard Beckwith say, "Yes, it is a great pity that the city is changing. Do you know, Poe, when I first

59

came here just thirty months ago, family businesses such as those dominated this area." He pointed toward the two buildings directly across the street. At this point in Maiden Lane, the road was unpaved and uneven, embossed with frozen ruts caused by the heavy wagons pulled by dray horses and the large handcarts of delivery boys. "Take a look, Poe, at New York in transition," he said with such nostalgia that anyone listening would have thought the Police Superintendent was a lifelong resident of the city.

Poe saw a frame colonial-style house which probably once had been a private residence. Now instead of a single doorway there were two separate entrances, one to a shop for mending clothing and the other to a showroom for men's custom-made apparel. Across the top of the dual entrance was a plain painted sign in three-foot letters proclaiming G. BUCKLASS, TAILOR. 57. The upper floor was where the proprietor and his family lived. The adjoining building, two stories high, was a toy factory. Painted across the front was GUSTAVUS F. MAAS, TOYS AND FANCY GOODS, MANUFACTURERS AND IMPORTERS. 59.

"In all candor, Beckwith, I really cannot grasp your point," admitted Poe, shaken by his self-imposed frightening experience the moment before and not daring to guess.

"My remark is meant as a prophecy," replied Beckwith. "Until about five years ago this part of the city was largely residential, with several churches and only a few firms. I am merely predicting that family businesses such as the ones I just indicated are already obsolete and will be swept away by the commerce which governs the growth of this city. Real estate here is already skyrocketing in value."

"Do you think it a good thing?"

"That is immaterial, since what I think will not stop the inevitable," replied Beckwith. "In this case, I judge it in terms of my interests: How does this growth affect the police force? Will the population shift also rearrange the political patterns of the city? Should I use some of my capital to invest in real estate beyond the present confines of the city? Are the recent fires, which seem to be increasing, accidental or have they been set by hired incendiaries to, shall I say, accelerate the changes in this part of the city? It is now a fact that the Great Fire of 1845, which destroyed the area to the northeast of us, was started by arsonists."

By this time, the two men had walked the three blocks of Pearl Street, made a left, and were striding along Wall Street, which here declined gradually until it reached the East River. So narrow was the street that there was barely room for the pair to walk abreast on the sidewalk. Often one or the other had to give way to pedestrians coming in the opposite direction. Nevertheless, Wall Street was filled with peddlers, fruit hawkers, knife sharpeners, delivery men with their carts brimming with packages, merchants rapidly heading for a meal, and messenger boys gaiting along. There was an oyster stand on the corner, specializing in plates of bluepoints and saddle rocks.

"I have been in many places between here and Indiana, but New York has a most singular effect," Beckwith exclaimed. "There is something about this city which propels people to their destination, no matter how trivial the reason. It is as if the next place they would reach is their El Dorado, and if a moment were wasted in getting there all would be lost."

The writer was pleased that Beckwith mentioned El Dorado and, since he agreed, he remained silent.

"Tell me, Poe," said Beckwith, introducing an apparent non sequitur, "the word *Importers* on the toy seller's building at Fifty-nine Maiden Lane made me think of a commonality of all our subjects. Did you mark it?"

"I would think," the writer responded, "that you refer to the coincidence that all five—Robert Moran, Count Motier, Philip Lewissohn, and Sir Richard and Lady Madelyn Townshend— have either left or entered the country in the past two years."

"Did you know," Beckwith started, "that here at Water and Wall streets was housed the Stock Exchange? The building is now

61

called the Tontine Coffee House and is unsurpassed for its plain American fare. I think we will eat there."

"Beckwith, will you be offended if I ask you a question?" probed Poe.

"No, but it does not necessarily mean I will answer it, particularly if it is a personal one."

"This penchant you have for antecedents of places and things. Is it an avocation of yours?"

"Forgive me, Poe, I do apologize if I sound didactic at times. I know these things because anything which touches on the city affects me. For instance, to state that Pearl Street was once called Magazine Street because the Dutch stored their gunpowder there or that Mangin Street was named after the co-designer of City Hall may be pedantic. But supposing there were a series of crimes committed in the vicinity of Canal Street and the culprits quickly disappeared. I would know to search beneath the street because in earlier days that thoroughfare was a canal. These are the reasons for my historical eruptions."

The poet noted that, no matter how seemingly casual, Beckwith had a utilitarian purpose in everything he did. This thought was in Poe's mind when the Police Superintendent guided the author through the doors of the Tontine Coffee House.

It was 1:25 P.M. when they emerged from the restaurant. Beckwith wanted to walk to Hudson Square, some twenty blocks distant. He then considered the poet's recent illness and dismissed the idea. He needed Poe in his best condition for the night's venture he planned.

"Our appointment is for two o'clock," Beckwith said. "We will make it with time to spare if we take a cab." The other man nodded. Poe seemed to have slipped into a depression and was becoming progressively more morose. As Beckwith waited for a passing cab, he returned the salute of a policeman who was walking on the other side of the street and scrutinized a very grave Poe.

They had not spoken much during the meal. There was only one minor item, and that would have passed unnoticed if it were not for Beckwith's omnivorousness for detail. As Beckwith ordered, Poe became increasingly restive. A few moments later, he asked Beckwith if he would not mind changing tables; they were too near the kitchen and the noise was annoying. They moved to another empty table. The poet was lying. Why? What was it that bothered him? From the changed location Beckwith noted that in the prior spot Poe was directly aligned with a mirror. He then recalled that in the Fordham cottage he had not seen a single mirror. This was not unusual, since mirrors were expensive ornamental pieces that had no place in a poor home, but he now recalled there was not even a small one for shaving near the washbasin in the writer's bedroom. Beckwith mused that Poe could not abide seeing his own reflection. What else could it be? Yet the poet's features were appealing, and Beckwith could understand why women particularly would think him handsome. Was there no end to the strangeness of this man?

It was then the food had arrived, all of it in great profusion. There was a great dish of ham and one of cold veal, cut in large slices and heaped in a mound, wheat and rye bread, cheese cut into odd shapes, hot tea, a variety of fish caught in the harbor that morning, cold deviled eggs, and, afterward, an excellently flavored coffee accompanied by chocolate pastries and plain cakes.

Poe had eaten sparingly, as if it was enough that his sight had been compensated by this great feast instead of his appetite being satiated from his near starvation of the past weeks. Twice Beckwith had followed Poe's eyes, once as the poet furtively glanced toward a bottle of Madeira at another table and once as he looked askance in the direction of the mirror.

It was not long before a cab appeared. As Poe took the single step up into the completely enclosed, half-sized coach with two wheels on either side so large that their rims reached the height of the side windows, Beckwith called "Hudson Square" to the driver, who was seated on the roof. The cab went up Wall Street and onto Broadway. As it made a left turn at Dey Street, Beckwith asked, "Are you not at all curious about where we are going?"

"As I am beginning to know you, I would say that you will reveal that at an appropriate moment," Poe replied.

"We are going to the home of Henry Schuyler, grandson of General Schuyler, nephew of Alexander Hamilton, and father of the deceased Alicia Schuyler, the second victim of the Garroter. Mr. Schuyler has agreed to cooperate by permitting the use of his home to gather our subjects. In this manner, we may see them and observe their dispositions. And the questioning will be done in a congenial environment so as not to arouse their suspicions."

"I agree," said Poe dully, who was now becoming peevish because he could detect no flaw in Beckwith's reasoning.

"Our five subjects plus the three girls, Misses Livingston, Jay, and Lewissohn, should be present," Beckwith continued. "This will probably be our only opportunity to interview them collectively. I am hoping that we may be able to pick up apparent contradictions while they are all together. In any case, it should be interesting."

The cab turned right onto Greenwich Street, went thirteen blocks, made another right, and stopped at the intersection of Beach and Hudson streets. On the official city map the single thoroughfare was designated Hudson Square, but because the area was dominated by the 214-foot spire of St. John's Chapel, to city dwellers it was known as St. John's Park. The wealthy had built spacious, three-storied, red-brick homes on the periphery of the park. Eventually, park and churchyard became noted for the variety and beauty of their trees.

"That will be eighty-five cents, sirs," the cabdriver announced.

"That will not be eighty-five cents but seventy cents," contradicted the Police Superintendent. "You did not take the direct route to Hudson Square. You should have taken the shorter route, which would have been from Wall to Broadway onto Walker, leading directly onto Beach. Therefore I give you the fare you are entitled to, sixty cents; the extra ten cents is for your agility at handling your vehicle in the heavy traffic. You should keep to that skill, driver, for you are not adept at cheating your passengers."

The cab went off without a protest from the driver. Poe thought, This Beckwith would waste substantial money on a meal, for undoubtedly he paid for many dishes he knew would not be eaten, but makes a point of disputing an overcharge of 15 cents. He is indeed a strange man.

In the open area of the park, the investigators felt the crisp wind which sought out and swirled the stray autumnal leaves. Even if the author had not been there the previous June for a reading of his poetry, he would know their destination by the black-creped doorway on the third home from the corner.

"We have four minutes before our interrogation," said Beckwith, opening his greatcoat, taking out his pocket watch, and checking it with the steeple clock. "Have you any thoughts before we enter? Anything I can elaborate on? Or perhaps there is something that *you* care to tell me?"

Poe looked intently at his companion. He thought the last question peculiar. Again, he pondered the doubt which had been forcing its way to the fore since he first met the man. Beckwith is something like me. His mind is not indentured to the ordinary. What is it exactly that he wants of me?

The moment passed and Beckwith swung the U-shaped brass knocker, so large and highly polished that Poe saw in it a distorted reflection of himself. His elongated head filled the right end and his stretched neck curved to meet his thin torso, which curved to his spindly legs and filled the other end of the U. It seemed Beckwith hit the knocker so hard that Poe could follow the inordinately loud sound in its rectangular path, in a complete circuit, around St. John's Square back to its point of origin. And in the three times that Beckwith made the motion, Poe saw himself three times slammed against the white door.

6

DECEMBER 1846

NEW YORK CITY
(St. John's Park)

After the liveried servant took their coats, Henry Schuyler came from a room on the left. Poe had only seen him from a distance, but he did know that the short, bearded man who had been the patriarch of this Knickerbocker family since the death of Alexander Hamilton did not approve of him.

Evidently the meeting had been discussed with Beckwith beforehand, for Schuyler did not seem surprised to see the writer. The welcome Poe received from the father of the dead girl was more cordial in tone, the poet knew, than it would have been under other circumstances.

"They are all here as you requested, Hollis, except for the British envoy and his wife," Schuyler almost whispered. "I regret that my wife cannot be present. She is still under a doctor's care. I can supply any detail from this house."

"Mrs. Schuyler's presence will not be needed, sir," Beckwith replied.

"Are there any new developments?" asked Schuyler.

"I am sorry there is nothing to report," responded the Police Superintendent. "I am sure that this is painful for you. If you wish to leave after the introduction . . ."

"No, I want to be present. I want to hear it all and see if I can possibly be of further service."

"Very well. I think we can proceed now."

Schuyler led them to a door on the left. The large room, like the house, reflected elegance. Two huge windows looked onto Laight Street and St. John's Park. Against the far wall there was a white marble fireplace with the chiseled figures of two cherubs with upraised arms at either end reaching up to support the notched white mantel, on which stood an elaborate candle holder. Covering the width of the fireplace and rising twelve feet from the mantel to the ceiling was a mirror adorned on either side by miniature Ionian marble columns.

Poe was amused to see a statue of Pallas on a stand in the near corner, a fad he had spawned since it was featured as a prop in "The Raven." Then came the realization that here again was something he had created that others had profited by while he received nothing. With this acerbic thought, he went into the room, avoiding the mirror's gaze.

Seated together on one section of an ottoman were two girls, with another young lady on a chair. This group of three sprang up, almost in unison, as the men entered the room, and the poet brightened as his name was the one pronounced.

"They told us you would be here, Mr. Poe, and we could scarcely believe it," said Priscilla Livingston.

"I heard you were quite ill, Mr. Poe. I am so glad to see you about," a sincerely concerned Joan Jay said.

"I do hope you can help with this terrible tragedy," exclaimed Sarah Lewissohn, with more emotion than she could contain, tears forming in her eyes.

This was followed by an outflow of questions from the young ladies to the poet.

"Please, Sarah, there is no need for more tears," Henry Schuyler kindly admonished. "There has been enough weeping in this house. Young ladies, you all know Mr. Poe, but I do not believe any of you have met Mr. Beckwith, our Police Superintendent. Mr. Beckwith, may I present Miss Joan Jay."

Joan Jay curtsied and thought, He does not at all fit the harsh things said about him. He is trim, though, and his eyelashes are long. Still, he would be more attractive if his eyes were blue instead of green.

"Miss Sarah Lewissohn."

Sarah Lewissohn curtsied and thought, He is better looking than my cousin Philip but not as handsome as Paul Motier. Whatever else, he certainly does not look like a policeman.

"Miss Priscilla Livingston."

Priscilla Livingston gave a slight curtsy and thought, His eyes are cool. He is taking in every part of me. Being in his presence stirs me; God, he has a virile quality. I wonder what he would be like in bed? Since I cannot have the man of my desires, what difference does it make? I think I would dare, but would he?

Beckwith saw three young ladies similar in appearance and age. They were pretty but probably bland New York society girls, and he dismissed any other notion. He was being unfair, he knew, with this collective judgment, but any other thought would be imprudent. They might need protection, but he doubted it. His warning to their families that they were not to be left unescorted would suffice. He had better ways to deploy his understaffed department.

Schuyler next introduced Poe and Beckwith to Robert Moran. They received a perfunctory greeting.

Poe: *Why are the rich aristocrats I meet invariably slim? Do they expend their energy accumulating money, counting it, or making sure they keep it? He is right-handed. How he fondles that cigar! Lactation? His demeanor conveys an assurance bordering on ennui. Does that go with being rich? Certainly helps. His eyes make unfeigned mockery of everything. Hair unfashionable, cut short. That streak of gray is too even. How clean-shaven he is, even at this time of day. His face is so bare, looks like the hairs have been plucked from each pore. Impeccably dressed. His boots have an extra heel. Pity money can't buy height. His walking stick beside him. It is a sword cane. He has no need of it in the middle of the day. That longish nose, the unwavering eyes, the square jaw. Yes, he is quite capable of using that sword cane.*

Beckwith: *He is trim. I will probably have to exercise twice as hard to have Moran's figure when I am in my forties. He exudes confidence. Or is it boredom? Or arrogance? He flicks his ash into the tray without turning his head yet never misses. Blunt fingers for so short a man. Pinkish fingernails, look sterilized. Probably has a pedicure done as well. Metallic eyes, gleaming with sustained amusement. Nose gives him hawkish appearance. No trace of beard. The whiteness on his chin is out of place for this time of day. Looks like no blood circulates in this area. Immaculate, as if he had just completed his toilet. A sword cane. Poe carries one, but he can only afford one stick. If I anger Moran, I will have to watch that right hand and cane. Probably not quick-tempered. Does not go with the self-assured disposition. Moran would have the wit to control delicate situations. I am sure, though, he would have no compunction about using that weapon if necessary.*

The poet and the Police Superintendent were then introduced to Philip Lewissohn. His tone was pleasant but insipid.

Poe: *He looks the merchant. Clothes respectable but hardly flattering. Probably unconcerned when being fitted and tailor took advantage. Flabby. Hair too curly for a man. Fair looking for a Jew. Peculiar. Has no Teutonic accent. Also wears no rings or jewelry, unlikely for an importer of precious stones. Large brown eyes. Suited for mooning. He glances in her direction even now as he makes the obligatory conversation. His fingers out of joint with the rest of him. Long and narrow. Appear strong. Being a pianist might account for it. I would not be gripped in anger by those hands.*

Beckwith: *Same height as Poe. Otherwise as opposite as men could be. Needs more exercise or he will soon put on much weight. Obsessed with his young lady. Tries but cannot keep his furtive eyes from Miss Livingston. Strange he has no accent. The Lewissohns never saw their nephew before he came to America. Must check my German contacts. Graceless movement for a gentleman. He is perhaps too obvious. A performance to disguise dexterity? Those fingers do not match his physique. If any trouble with him, must keep beyond arm's length.*

As he was appraising Philip Lewissohn, Beckwith heard the scraping of metal on the cobblestones. Without turning, he was able to see through the large window which looked out onto Laight Street.

The winter had been as bitter as any since Beckwith had come to the city three years before. There had been several ice and snow storms, starting in early November. Now, however, there was hardly enough ice in the street to warrant using a horse-drawn sleigh. Nevertheless, if the Townshends wished to use that open vehicle to display their hardiness, it was their business. The important thing was that they had come. If they had chosen not to, even as Police Superintendent he could do nothing. Diplomatic immunity and the influence of the world's greatest power protected them both. And Beckwith was sure it was the British couple. Even at that distance he could see she was a statuesque woman, an appearance enhanced by the full-length Russian sable coat and Cossack-style hat she was wearing. Beckwith mused that if enough ladies who set the fashions of the city were to see that sable outfit, John Jacob Astor would undoubtedly add to his already considerable fortune.

During the introduction to Paul Motier, the brass knocker sounded again.

Poe: *Our count is a pretty one. How he peacocks. Even in his slightest motion he struts upon this stage. In truth, it must be admitted Motier can afford to be vainglorious. Fine build, fine hands. Charming accent. Expensively dressed, but without the mannerisms of a fop. I never met anyone who bristles arrogance as he does. It would be to Motier's advantage to be skilled in dueling. He would appear to offend easily and to be easily offended.*

Beckwith: *He is overdone in every respect. Unappealing except perhaps to inexperienced females. A veritable rooster. How he*

70

radiates insolence. An example of European aristocracy at its worst. An insecure young man, however able he is to care for himself. If this Frenchman is as hot-tempered as reported, he could be a tiresome troublemaker.

The late arrivals entered the room. Schuyler went forward to greet Sir Richard and Lady Madelyn Townshend and, since they knew everyone else in the room, introduced them to Poe and Beckwith.

Poe: *She is sturdy. Fine English features, but without delicacy. She reeks health most unnaturally. She is taller than all of us except Beckwith. Such bearing. I fear she is obdurate. Our Police Superintendent is wrong; she would harm no one. She is lovely. Yet I would not have her. She should be dark and fragile. If she were so, I would want her. Ah, lady without bodily imperfection! What would it be to have such a woman? No, she is not my type. Still, I would make her the exception. I would have her if fate would have it so.*

Beckwith: *She is robust. How erect she stands despite her height. A proud carriage. I never thought brown hair attractive before. Nor that those high-neck dresses could ever be so deficient in masking a woman's figure. A man could revel in those breasts. Her frame could be mistaken for that of a man. Her strength probably could easily break another woman. She is different. I would want her if the circumstances were otherwise. Madelyn, if you were available I would try any ploy to have you.*

The pair then turned their attention to Sir Richard.

Poe: *Ruddy complexion. Immaculately attired, as is proper for a good English officer. It is no wonder that he was selected by his Queen for this position. Too mannered, though. And his eyes are cold. As if, like me, he has seen death many times. But then he is an accomplished duelist as well as a soldier. He stands close to his wife, not at all bothered that he is shorter. He has pride.*

Beckwith: *Excellent deportment. How dapper, like Van*

Buren. Every movement seems as calculated as if it were a battle
maneuver. But that is expected from a career military officer. Alert
eyes. He examines me as closely as I scrutinize him. Yes, he would
be a dangerous adversary on the dueling ground. If I had any
serious thoughts of trifling with his wife I would dismiss them now.

"Ladies and gentlemen," Schuyler began, silencing the conversations in the room. "I hope I have not inconvenienced you by asking you here this afternoon, but the Police Superintendent thought it might prove useful."

"Nonsense, Henry," Moran interjected. "Nothing is more important than resolving this horrid business."

"Mr. Beckwith is here," Schuyler continued, "in hopes that in discussing this matter together we might provide him with some detail which will lead him to this madman."

"More likely an excuse for staying indoors on a cold day rather than being in the street where the criminals are," commented Motier petulantly.

"Oh, Paul, can't you see that Mr. Beckwith is trying to do his job?" asked Priscilla Livingston.

"My wife and I will gladly do anything to aid this investigation," Townshend volunteered.

Beckwith commenced. "There are others who have been questioned and will be reexamined, but all here were with the Garroter's two victims during a critical time; that is, just before they were abducted. Was there anything unusual about the behavior of Miss Van Cortlandt or Miss Schuyler during that period? It does not matter how minor the detail may seem."

"You realize, Mr. Beckwith," Philip Lewissohn pointed out, "that we here were not in the habit of seeing each other regularly except for the girls. We only gathered as a group for occasions of a cultural nature, along with several others who had the same interest."

"I am aware of that, Mr. Lewissohn," Beckwith replied, "but you must also recall that Miss Van Cortlandt was murdered after just such an occasion, and that another literary gathering was scheduled on the evening that Miss Schuyler was murdered."

"So you are making a connection between our group and the murders," Moran concluded.

"I was hoping to discover something substantial by questioning the people who were with the Garroter's two victims," responded Beckwith, skirting the question.

Quickly changing the subject, the Police Superintendent went on without pause. "Then I take it none of you noted any peculiar actions by the deceased young ladies preceding their disappearance. They did not seem upset, exhibit uncharacteristic behavior, or mention anything untoward?" Beckwith searched for a reaction; there was none.

"Very well, then," he continued, striving to be casual with his next question. "I wonder if you could tell me where you were at the time that Miss Schuyler disappeared three days ago?" He looked first in Moran's direction.

"I was not feeling well that day and decided to leave my office early," the banker said. "I did not wish to be disturbed so I dismissed my servant for the day."

"And you, Mr. Lewissohn?"

"I went walking," the gem dealer answered. "I must admit it is something I don't usually do, but I felt particularly anxious that day and decided to do something different."

"And you, Count Motier?"

"I had no engagements so I spent that entire afternoon in my rooms."

Without waiting to be asked, Sir Richard said, "My wife and I were home. I don't recall going out at all. Am I remembering correctly, my dear?" Lady Townshend nodded in assent.

Poe listened to the interrogation in silence. And why should he say anything? he asked himself. He was accorded no official status. It was Beckwith's investigation; let him conduct it. My chance will come later. The poet did note, though, that none of the five subjects could prove their whereabouts during the hours of Alicia Schuyler's disappearance. However, it was Beckwith's intent that this interview was to be a prod, not a probe, the writer reminded himself, which was probably why his colleague was not pressing the point.

"Then there is nothing anyone can contribute which could be of possible value?" reiterated Beckwith. Joan Jay was becoming increasingly restive. Her fingers reached out and gripped Priscilla Livingston's hand.

"Yes, Miss Jay. Is there something you wish to tell me?" Beckwith asked softly.

The young girl became more agitated when she discovered that all of them were staring at her. Madelyn Townshend rose, walked over, and took her hand. As she gently stroked it, the Englishwoman spoke. The voice was deep and throaty, but kind. "My dear, if there is something that would help the Police Superintendent, you really should tell him."

"I suppose so," Joan Jay said, visibly upset. "It is just that I'm unsure and don't want anyone to get into trouble needlessly. Oh, Paul, you know I don't wish you any harm, but Alicia told me earlier that afternoon that she was going to meet you in the park at four o'clock."

The hour the Schuyler girl vanished, Poe recalled.

"Alicia said her father disapproved of Paul as a suitor," Joan Jay continued. "And since she wasn't sure she loved him she was going off to meet him on her own and make her own judgment."

"What do you say to that, Count?" Beckwith asked.

"I say that it is none of your business," the Frenchman responded angrily. "How dare you, a petty police official, interrogate me in this manner?"

"If you do not answer the question, Count, this petty police official will see that you are jailed and then deported," Beckwith bluffed.

"Well, if you must know," Motier answered, becoming even more infuriated at being successfully intimidated. "Miss Schuyler and I arranged a rendezvous so that for once we could be alone.

74

To, shall I say, explore each other's feelings. But I fell asleep and arrived at the park late. She never appeared. I assumed, when I did not see her, that she had returned home."

"It would have been better if you had volunteered this information," Beckwith said.

"Who are you to address me in this rude manner?"

"I thought you made that apparent. I am a petty police official. Surely they have them in France."

"They do, but I was never exposed to them," Motier enunciated slowly to emphasize his distaste. "And if I had been, I assure you they would not have dared to treat me so in my own country."

"I would remind you that you are not in your own country," was Beckwith's rejoinder. "In any case, you would be correct. You would not be treated so in France. Louis Philippe's rule is egalitarian—tyranny and injustice to all. The Citizen King jails workers as well as Bourbons, any who oppose him. The Citizen King—what a farcical title!"

"You insult my country," retorted Motier, being deliberately provocative.

"It is strange that you defend one who is the political enemy of your family," Beckwith noted. "Besides, I was not the one to bring up this subject."

"Now you insult me, Monsieur Beckwith."

"That is not my intent," replied the police official with equanimity. Motier is trying to draw you in and you are deftly sidestepping him, Poe observed. But instead of further mollifying the hothead, Beckwith added, "One might observe, Count, that you insult easily."

"Superintendent, I consider that remark one which demands satisfaction and to make my point I now formalize my indignation." Before anyone could stop him, Motier reached across, snatched the gloves Townshend had fastidiously laid across the arm of his chair, and slapped Beckwith across the face with them.

The three young ladies gasped, Philip Lewissohn paled, a sardonic grin came across Moran's face, Sir Richard appeared impassive, and Lady Townshend's eyes brightened with interest.

"Count Motier, I really must protest," Schuyler said, outraged. "How dare you violate the hospitality of my home with this boorish display? Also, the laws of this state prohibit dueling."

"I apologize for any disrespect, Monsieur Schuyler, but I am entirely justified," Motier responded. "I will not be insulted, no matter the circumstances."

"Paul, you stop this nonsense," said Priscilla Livingston. "Take back your challenge or I will never speak to you again."

"I cannot and I will not. An insult calls for satisfaction."

"The young man is quite right, Miss Livingston," Beckwith interposed. "Insults demand response and arrogance deserves recognition. Those who are not competent to cope with insult by wit must compensate by other means."

Motier's face grew livid and Poe thought he would leap forward in fury, but the Frenchman's eyes distended and he said, "My seconds will call upon you within twenty-four hours."

"One moment, Count. What weapons are to be used?" Beckwith queried.

"I leave that to you," replied the cocky Motier.

"Very well. The long rifle. You may have heard it called the Mississippi or Yager rifle. Or if you wish to use a European equivalent of this fifty-four-caliber weapon, I have no objection. But take care that it has a range of four hundred yards, for that will be our firing distance. If we both miss, there will be no pause. There will be immediate reloading, and the first man ready will fire again."

"Impossible. Who ever heard of a duel with rifles? It is not gentlemanly."

"This is America, Count. We have restructured chivalry here, and there are many rules concerning the code duello you probably never heard of. For example, I am also taking advantage of 'Smythe's 1826 Addendum' to the 1763 version of *Burke's*

76

Rules of Dueling Adhered to by Colonial Gentlemen on the North American Continent."

"And that would be?" Motier asked, his curiosity overcoming his rage.

"That if one of the participants in a duel is an established resident of the area where the contest is to take place, he may set aside sixty days to arrange his affairs before taking part in the duel."

"And what, sir, is the logic behind that delaying codicil?"

"Why, Count, that is perfectly obvious. America is primarily a nation of entrepreneurs, not of gentlemen of leisure. It takes a businessman a considerable time to settle his affairs. We Americans must make sure everything is in order if we know our end is coming. Surely sixty days is a reasonable time to call in notes, make wills, settle estates, dispute with lawyers about their fees, and be concerned with all the matters relevant to a man's dying. It makes sense if you just think how long it takes after a man's death to unravel his affairs. Poe, you are an expert on the code duello of all nations. Is not 'Smythe's Addendum' still in force?"

The poet was so fascinated by the sheer idiocy of Beckwith's dialogue that the question almost unbalanced him. He had not heard such nonsense outside his satirical stories. Recovering quickly, he took up his sponsor's cue.

"What you say is quite valid," Poe adjudicated. "I know of nothing that has superseded 'Smythe's Addendum.' "

"Therefore," Beckwith continued, "I take advantage of it and set the date of our engagement at any time after sixty days hence."

"You think you cozen me, but I do not accept this delay," replied the furious Motier. "I will not be balked."

"Then perhaps I can accommodate you," Sir Richard said quietly.

"What's this, what's this?" exclaimed a thoroughly perplexed Motier, turning in the direction of the diplomat, who remained seated. "I have no quarrel with you, sir."

77

"But I have one with you," Townshend replied, staring at the young noble. "I do not care for other persons to handle my apparel. You did not ask my permission, sir, to use my gloves. I dislike others using my personal items for purposes I do not deem suitable, particularly when they touch them to another person."

"But I did not realize you would be offended—"

"It seems you do not allow for intentions," interrupted Sir Richard. "Of course, Mr. Beckwith has precedence in this matter. If he wishes to defer to me, I can give you the duel you seem so anxious to have, with the weapons you prefer. Pistols at close quarters or swords and at your convenience. Tomorrow, if that suits you."

Schuyler was once again protesting and the others were stunned into silence by this new turn.

To Poe it was obvious what the English diplomat was doing. He was blatantly telling the Frenchman either to accept Beckwith's condition of a sixty-day delay or face the prospect of an immediate duel with a more deadly adversary.

Motier surveyed his exacerbating situation. He now had the prospect of two duels: one with an experienced man—for he knew Sir Richard's reputation—and, if he survived that engagement, the next with an opponent who would use a weapon he had had little opportunity to practice with, the long rifle. He was neither a coward nor stupid. He would need time to prepare. The Count came to his decision.

"My quarrel is not with you, sir, but with this insensitive policeman. I accept the deferment, but I insist that the duel take place at the end of the prescribed period."

"That is very gracious of you, Count Motier," responded Beckwith. "To consummate the agreement would you kindly step over here?"

What the devil is Beckwith up to now? Poe wondered. It would really be a gauche American gesture if his associate were to shake hands with this arrogant foreigner. Poe was becoming embarrassed for his companion as the young Frenchman sauntered over.

"Do I have your word as a gentleman that you will hold off this duel for at least sixty days?" Beckwith was being unduly rhetorical, Poe thought.

"I believe that was settled," Motier impatiently affirmed.

"I just wanted to be sure you understood the agreement and that everyone in the room was a witness to it," Beckwith declared. "Undue emphasis on corroborating statements is a professional fault of mine. And because, Count, I wish nothing to disturb our agreement. You see, you have an advantage and I thought I would even it."

Beckwith's left hand moved so fast that Poe barely saw his arm go forward. The open palm struck Motier full on the cheek. The Frenchman went sprawling backward across the room, upsetting a small table with a vase of flowers and the stand with the bust of Pallas, which smashed when it hit the floor. As Motier sat up, dazed, five red marks appeared on his cheek.

"I thought, Count, that as long as we are going to have a duel there should be sufficient reason *for me* to participate."

Motier made an effort to rise and attack, but he was too stunned.

"Ah, sir, I beg you to remember your promise, which was heard by all here. Besides, Count, there is no humiliation involved and none intended. You struck me once and I struck you once. It is our Christian obligation to turn the other cheek. However, the Bible does not specify that both cheeks must necessarily be on the same face.

"And now, I must be leaving. I am grateful, ladies and gentlemen, for your cooperation. Of course, I reserve the right to interview you individually, though I doubt if it will be necessary. Please be so kind as to inform me if you intend to leave the city. Thank you again and good afternoon."

And with a slight bow Beckwith left the room. Poe lingered a moment and approached Townshend, although his eyes involuntarily went again to his wife. "That was a gallant gesture to rescue my friend, Sir Richard. I wish to thank you on his behalf."

"Your colleague seems quite capable of taking care of himself, Mr. Poe," the Englishman said firmly. "Besides, it was as stated: I do not care for anyone to handle anything of mine. However, if you wish to interpret it otherwise, so be it."

"Nevertheless, I am sure I speak for Mr. Beckwith when I say he is most appreciative," persisted Poe, whose thought about the possible death of his source of easy income on the morrow was commingled with a sincere concern for Beckwith's safety.

Poe hurried out to catch up to the Police Superintendent, but he was preceded into the hallway by Schuyler, who was conversing with Beckwith as the servant got their coats.

"Hollis, I am worried about you. Motier is most undisciplined. Otherwise I could not have been more delighted to see that strutting popinjay smashed. He would never be in this house were it not for this exceptional occasion. He shall never enter here again."

"I am sorry to have caused this disturbance in your home," Beckwith responded. "But as long as he insisted on a duel I thought there should be good reason for having one. I would be pleased if you were to tally the cost of the damage and send me the bill."

"Nonsense, Hollis, I will do no such thing. It was delightful, better than watching Edwin Booth in *Othello*. It is worth the price at twice the cost."

Poe and Beckwith then went out the door in the direction of Canal Street, the writer having difficulty keeping up with the Police Superintendent's quick-march step.

"Sorry to hurry you, Poe, but I want to get away from here quickly, before that volatile Frenchman changes his mind. When he cools, he will be persuaded to keep the agreement. Whatever else, we did find out the answer to the question of whether he is crafty or has excellent advisers. I would categorically say it was the latter."

"Beckwith, what was that nonsense back there about Smythe and Burke? You know that no American manual on dueling exists."

"Of course I do," Beckwith averred. "And I thank you for picking up on it. As a matter of fact, I got the idea from your story 'Mystification.' The one in which the noble deliberately provokes the lout into a duel. Then Von Jung, if I remember correctly, gets out of it by relying on the stupidity of his rival, who professes to be an authority on dueling and does not wish to concede his ignorance of a point which Von Jung fabricates.

"I would have gladly given Motier his opportunity immediately, especially when it involves the long rifle, a weapon I am proficient with. However, the capture of the Garroter has priority over all, including pretentious injuries to petty vanities. With pistols or swords, the Count would have a chance of besting me. With a long rifle, he has practically none. Yet I cannot allow myself this indulgence while the Garroter is at large. All the threads of this disentanglement are in my hands. You know about as much as I do, but you have no official status. And probably no one would listen to you. The apprehension of our madman—for now he truly belongs to us—is paramount over imagined rufflings of honor, over personal considerations, over ambitions, over the code duello, that damned European importation!"

Poe's ego had again swelled when Beckwith mentioned another of his stories which now had become the mechanism for a successful ploy he actually witnessed. However, his vanity did not block his curiosity as to why Beckwith was such a devotee of his. "Mystification" was one of his minor works, published almost a decade before in the *American Monthly Magazine* as "Von Jung, the Mystific." It had been included in only one anthology published four years ago. Beckwith must have gone to considerable trouble to get a copy. A cab came, and his companion practically pushed the writer into it.

"We are going home, Poe, to assess our findings thus far. To Lafayette Place, driver, and take the direct route."

7

DECEMBER 1846

NEW YORK CITY
(Lafayette Place)

Poe had been active for nine consecutive hours and his energy expired. When Beckwith suggested that he rest in the guest bedroom, the writer gratefully accepted, despite its being only a quarter to three in the afternoon. He was now in a rigor mortis sleep of exhaustion, his position never changing and his breathing imperceptible.

This was after the cab had stopped on Lafayette Place in front of Beckwith's house. Poe had never been in that section of the city, but he knew it to be an enclave of affluence. Why had he not chosen to go into politics? Surely it was a career in which a clever man such as himself could become well off without difficulty. But as he descended the high step from the cab to the cobblestoned street his perspective was regained with his balance.

I am what I am because it is what I choose to be, Poe thought. If I had been obsequious to my foster father, I would be the master of a house such as this in Richmond. If I had stifled my desire to be a poet, I probably would have inherited a goodly portion of John Allan's fortune. If I had not infuriated him, if I had not forthrightly spoken against his shameful philandering and his neglect of my foster mother in her dying time, I too could afford Beckwith's style.

But in a vacillating thought, Poe reaffirmed his vow to his craft: My poetry is everything. To be in politics I would have had to be as mendacious as I would have been with my foster father. To grovel, to prostrate myself before the mob would be humiliating. One course would have been as bad as another. If only there were stricter copyright laws, I would have made my fortune by writing.

As Poe conjectured, the ire that was envy for Beckwith dissipated. Can I be angry at this man any more than at any other wealthy man? Beckwith may be my salvation. His influence can be useful. I am better off with him than without him. And there was something akin to affection in the poet as he glanced at his companion, who was opening the iron gate leading to his front door.

As Beckwith loosened his greatcoat to reach for his keys, there came over him a sense of disquietude. Something undefined bothered him. He then realized that despite the bright day that there was a slough of darkness caused by the huge Corinthian column, a dense shadow near the front door into which the sunlight dissolved. Beckwith had noted it before and it disturbed him. When he unlocked the door, his back was to that impenetrably black area. He was not one to make himself vulnerable, even in minute things. It was not the first time he had had this misgiving, but with Poe that ineffable feeling became sensitized. He had thought of placing a gaslight between the front entrance and the column. However, since he had many visitors after nightfall whom he did not wish to be visible to those who might be spying, he had left it the way it was.

Once inside, Beckwith offered Poe food, hot beverages, and a change of clothing. What the writer really wanted was a drink, but he knew that it was not worth even hinting at.

As Beckwith led him upstairs, Poe had a chance to scrutinize his surroundings. The interior of the house was meticulously clean, and there was not a superfluous piece of furniture. The total effect was one of impersonality.

In the bedroom Beckwith again offered the author a change of clothes. When the drawer was opened and Poe saw the smooth, creamy linen shirts, he was tempted. It had been so long since he had had a new shirt. However, his pride would not let him. He would steal before he would accept charity, and the offer was mutely refused.

Poe fell into a dreamless sleep, without despicable visages and phantasmagoric images. His deranged dreams had become so commonplace that the beasts in his mind no longer frightened him—he merely wondered what new shapes they would take.

In his somnolescence, the poet sensed movement which caused him to open his eyes. At least it was his thought that he willed them to open. In the transformation from blackness to the scene of a bedroom, he saw a pistol pointing at him. He was not taken aback, for he thought that the incursion into reality had not yet been completed. It was when Poe realized that he was fully awake and that the pistol was aimed at him, a finger cocking the hammer to fire, that he became startled. He leaped from the bed as he heard the click of the trigger.

"Poe, how thoughtless of me," Beckwith apologized. "Calm yourself. I came up and saw you still asleep and became absorbed with this Allen pepperbox. I had no idea that the slight noise would awaken you."

Poe soothed his raven hair with his hands as he walked across the room. There on the table were several pistols, mostly of the percussion type; he was more familiar with the flintlocks. There was a Hall, a Remington, a Derringer, and the .32-caliber Allen the Police Superintendent held in his hand. Then he noted the long-barreled .28-caliber Texas revolver with its hidden trigger and hinged-lever rammer. He had heard much about this new weapon, which had a revolving cylinder instead of revolving barrels as in a pepperbox. He had never seen one, for the Colt five-shooter was in great demand because of the war.

"Yes, the Texas revolver is hard to acquire," Beckwith commented, following Poe's gaze. "This one was confiscated in a drunken shooting case. The double action gives an edge in fire-power, but its disadvantages are its size and weight. Hardly a weapon for city folk. For accuracy, this is the one I favor." Poe recognized the Haston percussion two-shot.

Though often threatened with and threatening a duel, Poe had not handled a pistol in years, certainly not with the familiarity he had in his West Point days. There he had fired the now-obsolete .69-caliber Johnson and .54-caliber North.

"Come, Poe, to the cellar and the necessary preliminaries to this night's venture."

The cellar, the author observed, was oddly lacking in stored household paraphernalia. Curious also were the many gas lamps along the wall; in moments the cellar became as brightly lit as a dining room. It was then that he noticed various marks painted on the floor, the iron-shuttered windows, and sandbags piled against the far wall. The cellar was a pistol range. And the writer, who had an acute appreciation of the bizarre, was delighted.

"Choose one you feel comfortable with and fire whenever you care to," said Beckwith, as he fastened a paper target in the center of the sandbagged area.

This was an unexpectedly new turn and angst came upon the poet. I should tell him, Poe thought. But pride overcame all other considerations. The writer was anxious to display proficiency in all things and he determined to do his best. Nevertheless, he picked up the Haston without enthusiasm.

"Fifteen yards is a good starting point," Beckwith judged, handing him a small packet and taking out his watch. "Start whenever you wish."

Poe got the feel of the pistol and gripping it made him stand more erect. He aligned himself with the target and sighted in a few times. Then he indicated he was ready. He quickly bit off the end of powder-paper cylinder, took the ball and rammed it into the weapon, brought up the piece, aimed, and fired.

"Forty-five seconds," announced Beckwith, as he walked to examine the target. "You're just three inches off the mark. Most satisfactory for someone who has not shot for a long time." Actually, it was slow, but Beckwith noted that the poet's hand was much steadier than he had expected it to be, and the movements were sharp and correct; undoubtedly Poe's army training was responsible.

"Not bad," Beckwith reiterated, "but you must do better. Try again." This time the complete movement, from loading to firing, took about forty-one seconds and Poe's shot was two inches from the target's center.

"You're getting better, but it still will not do," Beckwith said. He gave the writer his watch, picked up a bottle, set it as a target, and walked back to the twenty-five-yard mark. Poe began the timing as Beckwith nodded his head. The bullets were rammed and fired. The first shot shattered the neck; the second shot demolished the bottle—done within ten seconds. It was a display of marksmanship Poe had rarely seen.

"I do not expect you to match that in the next hour," Beckwith said without modesty, "but you can do better since it is evident that you were once quite good. I will leave you here. Practice with the Haston. It will steady your aim. Then use the pepperbox, which you will carry tonight. Where we are going I would only feel safe with a musketoon; unfortunately, it would be too conspicuous."

Whatever Beckwith had in mind, Poe also preferred the musketoon (the Model 1816 he had trained with as a cadet). Then he would not have to go through this exercise in silliness, for the musketoon required little skill and its blast radiated. But despite his annoyance at this discipline, there was a masculine stirring of pride and his sad eyes glistened with satisfaction when, after moving back to the twenty-yard mark, he got off his third shot dead center.

Later, while Beckwith changed his clothes, Poe's only concession to his host's hospitality was to use his razor, for it was the poet's habit to shave before going out for the evening, no matter what the occasion. In passing the open door, Beckwith saw Poe turn away from the mirror in the bathroom, wet himself with basin water, apply the shaving soap, and dexterously sweep the sharp razor over his face as if he were actually seeing his reflection.

They left the house at 10:30 P.M. There was no difficulty in getting a cab, but the driver objected when told his destination was the Five Points. It was only by strenuous pressuring as the Police Superintendent that Beckwith induced the man to take them to Chatham Square.

The vehicle headed down Great Jones Street, making a right turn onto the Bowery. The cab's interior was dark, and neither man could see the other's features. Poe lifted his hand from his cane to his smooth face, satisfying himself that he had not missed a spot. In this shifting he felt an odd weight in the right pocket of his guardcoat. Yes, the pepperbox revolver, he reminded himself. In his left pocket was a cartouche box. Beckwith had not asked Poe about his marksmanship. His sole comment on the subject was to instruct the poet that should there be a situation requiring the pistols, the firing would be done in tandem. In this manner, Beckwith would get a chance to reload before Poe finished his five rounds.

The writer was now becoming increasingly aware of the city about him and eagerly sought information for a future prose work. For the American backdrop Poe had disdained as settings in his stories was now the stalking ground of the Garroter.

"Beckwith," Poe began, his words intruding into darkling silence, "when I came to New York I was particularly enjoined to keep away from the Five Points. This warning was repeated to me more than once by those who knew me to be a stranger to this city. I heeded this advice only because my interests did not incline in that direction. I never bothered to find out more. What exactly is the Five Points?"

"If God meant men to have a foretaste of Hell then the Five Points was created for that purpose. This Hell began as a pond called the Collect, used by the Dutch to water livestock. In the center of this large pond was an island used by the authorities for hangings, to burn the condemned at the stake, or to break men's bodies on the wheel. As Manhattan grew, the pond was covered over with dirt and built upon.

"The area became the Sixth Ward. Some distance to the southeast of the Collect there formed, where Orange, Cross, and Anthony streets intersect, a place resembling the center of a wheel from which five spokes radiate. Thus the name for this district became the Five Points.

"Then about twenty-five years ago the foundations of the clapboard houses and commercial buildings began to crack and sink, for the Collect had not been properly filled in. The lower classes began to congregate there because of the cheap rent, a trend abetted by the families fleeing the area as a stench seeped from the now marshy underground.

"Soon dance halls and bull-baiting pits opened. The green-grocers began to distill liquor at lower prices than the regular saloons. The backrooms of these greengroceries became the gathering place for thugs and hooligans, who organized into gangs.

"As time passed the area grew more malignant. The destitute, the outcast, the degenerate, the freed Negro, and the runaway slave possessed the place. This reputation, in turn, drew all classes of men who had the price to pay for its debaucheries. Some were men of good family and bright futures whose prodigal and dissolute natures brought them there.

"The centerpiece of this disreputable section is the Old Brewery, a dilapidated five-story structure. In it are about seventy-five rooms of various sizes, each filthier and more malodorous than the other. This rookery shelters about a thousand inmates, crowded together in the most deplorable conditions. Many have been within the Old Brewery much of their lives, for if one leaves his place unguarded it can be immediately claimed by another. If there is a contest, only death settles the dispute. I have heard of children born in the Old Brewery who have not seen sunlight; I have heard of a six-year-old girl who was bludgeoned to death for showing the penny she had begged. It is estimated that for the

88

past fifteen years there has been a murder a night in the Five Points.

"Poe, before I go further, I must caution you not to let your Southern upbringing override our safety, for there you will see Negroes cohabiting with whites. Make no comment! Many consider themselves married and are as protective of their families as you would be of yours. This I have seen with my own eyes, for there is a huge communal room on the first floor of the Old Brewery called the Den of Thieves, no doubt named by one of its more whimsical inhabitants."

This picture in his mind's eye disgusted Poe and he hotly exclaimed, "If you know all this, why do you not go and purge the district?"

"Because the Five Points is a warren with passages leading from building to building and hidden tunnels in which the hunted can scurry like rats. We have given up patrolling it, for two or three policemen are easy prey for the gangs. Last year, three of my men who had the courage to enter the area were murdered and their heads displayed on pikes. We can only go in, as we do from time to time, with a large force. But the narrow streets make us vulnerable, for when the gangs feel bold enough they attack even large numbers of police. In fact, along the Old Brewery there is a particularly narrow street called Murderer's Row which we are careful to avoid. There is another unholy byway named the Abbatoir, a cul-de-sac from which there is no exit for the stranger."

"But surely," asked Poe, "if this district is as abominable as you describe, why has it not been razed?"

"For several reasons," explained Beckwith. "In any city the poor must settle somewhere. There are many tenants who continue to pay rent to landlords, some of whom are our leading citizens. Also, the Old Brewery may be abandoned, but it is still the property of the Coulter family, who would gladly sell it. But who would purchase it? What kind of value does it have?"

"Then you have given these outlaws, these dregs, the victory," Poe protested, "for it appears they rule this part of New York."

"Except for an occasional foray with a large force and constant vigilance to assure that they do not move out of the Five Points in gangs, my reply to that is yes," the Police Superintendent said dispassionately. "There is nothing else to do but institute a *cordon sanitaire*. It would take an army the size of ours in Mexico to occupy the area. And what use would such a gesture be so long as the Five Points remains a region of deformed tenements and forsaken people? By the way, Poe, the gangs were not formed solely for profit. National pride is another basis for their existence."

"Oh, come now, Beckwith," responded the skeptical Poe, "that is too outlandish to believe."

"It is so, nevertheless. The most notorious gang is the Bowery Boys, or Bhoys, depending how Gaelic they feel when they are committing their felonies. This identification stems from the hostility of our city population to foreigners, particularly Irish Catholics. On the other hand, the True Blue Americans was formed as a patriotic counterpart. Imagine, Poe, Protestant street rabble protecting the American nation from insult. Then there are dissidents of these groups, the Dead Rabbits and the Plug Uglies, the Roach Guards and the Chichesters, each vying for supremacy over the Five Points, each forming coalitions periodically with the others to achieve that goal. Does it not sound familiar? Would not Albany or Washington be a more fitting environ for such dealings? But the battleground here, more often than not, is the open space called Paradise Park. And, Poe, there is full equality here. Many of the women take part with the men in their bloody feuds. The more dedicated have sharpened their teeth and hurl themselves into a fight with knives flying. These females would sooner slash the guts of an opponent than caress their gangster lovers."

The cab stopped suddenly, unseating both men. A dog had

wandered into the path of the cab and the horse's hoof had struck it, sending the bleeding animal howling into the night.

"These things you relate are quite unbelievable," Poe said.

"They are true nonetheless," replied Beckwith.

"I have never heard them spoken of," the writer persisted.

"Respectable citizens shun this place; others are perhaps ashamed that such an abomination exists within their city. Apart from my official position, I have never heard the Five Points spoken of either."

"Then why in God's name are we going there?" Poe blurted out.

"The Garroter, of course. Where else is the devil more likely to be found but in Hell?" responded Beckwith.

The cab stopped and the men alighted. That he was beside the Police Superintendent of the City of New York did not comfort Poe, and as they walked his eyes scanned each foot of Orange Street.

"Let us suppose that the Garroter is not one of the five persons we have considered. Let us suppose he is a madman. I think you would agree that this person would feel safer within the Five Points. His aberrant behavior would not be questioned. I am here to find out if such a person is in this area."

"And shall we do this by walking up and down the streets and peering in each hovel until we note such a personage?" asked a dour Poe.

"Why not?" replied Beckwith. "Did not your protagonist do that in 'The Man of the Crowd'? However, it will be unnecessary. I have a reliable informer who will pass information to me."

"Then why is our presence required?"

"My informer is of the Five Points, a member of one of the gangs. He came to my home just yesterday for instructions after the second murder. He is in a dangerous position as it is. To absent himself again so soon would mark him. He is a valuable agent. I cannot endanger the source of such intelligence, nor would I needlessly risk the life of anyone in my employ. He is my obligation."

I, too, am your obligation, Poe thought, and yet here I am.

"My informer is to meet me tonight," Beckwith continued. "Since he cannot leave the district without danger, I come in— as I have done twice before."

The two men walked several hundred feet north until they came to an open area. Poe looked about and shuddered. He stood in the rotary of evil, the Five Points.

8

DECEMBER 1846

NEW YORK CITY
(The Five Points)

It was not what Poe had anticipated. True, there was an unclean pall which hung heavy in the streets. The buildings were warped and tumid: roofs were collapsed like men with their heads bashed in, entrances were concave gashes resembling shadowy rictus. Poe had expected a mephistic aura, but there was only a slight aroma of decay.

Yet there were people about, casual in their postures, sauntering as if they were shoppers on Broadway. The writer saw men promenading with well-dressed ladies. From their clothes, he knew that the women were from bordellos in the better part of the city, accompanying escorts who came for the salacious divertissements of the Five Points. Nevertheless, he was fearful.

"No need to be apprehensive, Poe. You are safer by being classed a tourist."

"Why is that?" shot back Poe, piqued once more that his companion probed his thoughts.

"For the reason which underlines almost all our American motives, economics. There is an enforced code of hospitality which protects the stranger here. Five Points indigents are expendable and are permitted to kill one another with impunity. However, the stranger is looked on as the source of prosperity, whose money makes this area flourish. Recognizing this, the heads of the greengroceries, the dance halls, and the whorehouses have decreed safe-conduct to all strangers. Is this not entrepreneurial acumen?

"Of course, all events here cannot be controlled. That is not possible even in our nearly perfect society. Men get unruly and women become cantankerous. The results can be fatal to both the resident and the tourist. Still if one behaves and does not offend another, the best protection is this code. For instance, Poe, should we enter a place here, as we will, the custom calls for us as gentlemen to buy drinks for all present. But supposing we were robbed of our money or murdered as we crossed into this district. Think of the many who would be deprived of this sustenance. Only our despoiler would profit. However, in our generosity the commonwealth of the Five Points benefits.

"Still, there are the criminally unpredictable who cannot control their passions. Therefore, our weapons. Also, if my identity as a policeman were revealed, we would not be spared. Nor does the code protect Englishmen from the Kerryonians, a gang of men from County Kerry. They are fanatics in the cause of Irish independence and think the best way to achieve this is to murder British nationals."

This narration did little to reassure Poe. However, he grew calmer as he noted the dress and heard the speech of the passersby. Many were gentlemen.

Suddenly, he was yanked from his feet by an arm gripping him. The surge of terror subsided when the writer realized it was his companion forcing him into the shadows. Beckwith indicated that he should look across the street.

"Confirm it," Beckwith whispered. "Is that not John Moran?"

There was no mistaking the small banker, moving smoothly along the opposite sidewalk, a petite brunette holding his arm.

"I suppose he is entitled to his pleasures," said Poe. "If

Moran does not wish the company of a respectable lady, then that is his affair."

"Certainly, Poe. However, that is no lady accompanying him. In fact, I doubt if it is a woman."

Startled, the poet looked again as the pair passed under a gas lamp. Poe had keen eyes. The self-conscious movements of the young body, the overdone cosmetics, the uneasy garments, the slim buttocks. He had read about this desecration many times, but never had he seen a sodomite.

"Moran's mistress is a catamite," Beckwith confirmed. "Now we know why our solitary banker does not allow females or their representation in his home."

"Do you think Moran is the Garroter?" Poe asked. "No doubt he hates women. And he walks with ease in the Five Points."

"That may well be true," Beckwith conjectured. "However, in my opinion, a misogynist would have chosen his victims haphazardly. The Garroter killings form a definite pattern. If the motive was unadulterated hatred, why the elaborate rituals with the victims? This is what we must disentangle. Also, Moran has found outlet for his particular sexual expression. In my observation of criminals, it is only when a man is thwarted in releasing his desires that he strikes out in fury. Moran has found a mode to maintain his equilibrium. Still, there is no predicting the behavior of a deviant. Moran now becomes a prime suspect."

They continued walking east on Cross Street, now nothing more than a muddy slurry. Every other storefront seemed to be either a grocery or a saloon. From a distance Poe saw that the outsiders were milling about a festering brick structure, undoubtedly the Old Brewery. There were crowds on all sides, a mosaic of bodies, a pastiche of gestures. Some were bold enough to step within the narrow opening of a nine-foot wall stretching along the right side of the building. Men were whispering into the ears of women, adolescents in filthy rags scurried about begging, and comely children were being held in the air for appraisal.

Poe beheld this marketplace of lechery, this obscene agora, and gripped his cane in rage. This was the result of the contagion of Northern democracy. Such a vile place would never be tolerated in the ordered society of the South. There, each had his station, each would be cared for, no matter how menial his rank, no matter his color. However, for Poe, the Five Points represented more than anything else the luridness of reality. The hot moment passed and he felt a huge sadness for all within this charnel for the living. He was as poor as any there, yet he was fortunate. He could suffer his poverty in private.

Some yards before they came to the Old Brewery, Beckwith led him into a lane and to a three-story building with dormers. As they were descending into the cellar, Poe was able to read the battered sign, COW BAY ALLEY, THE BALLROOM OF MR. PETE WILLIAMS, ESQ., DECEASED, AT PRESENT CONDUCTED BY MR. PRITTIES, PROP.

They entered a large open room with a low ceiling made bright by hoop chandeliers filled with candles of whale oil and tallow. The cellar was bare except for long wooden benches and a few upturned barrels cut in half for use as seats. The only attempt at decoration was curtains of red bombazine, long unwashed. The wood floors were sanded, for better traction for the men with their heavy boots. In the corner, above a counter which served as a bar, was a dingy sign, DANCING FREE FOR CUSTOMER PURCHASE OF ONE ALE, PORTER, OR BEER. There was a stove at the far end of the room, with a pipe leading up and away through an opening in the window. The room was stifling and both men opened their coats. On the right, against the wall, was a platform on which were a hunched white man with a fiddle and a colored man with a banjo, playing at a frenzied pace.

The room was filled with perhaps thirty-five men and women of both races. Almost all the men wore soft felt hats and dirty jackets and trousers. In the center of the floor was a Negress wearing a soiled dress showing petticoats, with a little cigar in her mouth. A white man was her dancing partner. Almost everyone in the room was watching the couple in an endurance contest which had been going on for some time. The only oddity in the group, if anything in that setting could be called odd, the poet thought, was a white man whose small stature was accentuated by a large plug hat that was jammed down to his ears.

The music surprised Poe. It was an Irish jig, and intricate steps were being executed by the dancers. The boards creaked as the mixed couples kept their interminable pace to the Gaelic folk tune. The musicians tired first, and with a gesture of exhaustion they stopped—to the catcalls and threats of the onlookers. Their displeasure evaporated when Beckwith called out, "Drinks for all who care to have them and for all the drink of their choice." This was followed by cheers and a rush to the counter.

"The little man in the black plug hat is a member of the Plug Uglies," Beckwith said under his breath as he leaned forward to throw money on the counter. "The hat is stuffed with wool and leather to protect his head against blows." At that moment a nub of a man with a frayed face ambled over to Beckwith, holding his mug high. The froth from the ale had left a whitish residue on his upper lip.

"I am most grateful, sir," he said pleasantly. "This was an arid night until you came." And with that expression of appreciation he downed the remaining ale in a swallow and made his way to a corner, slipped down in a sitting position, and closed his eyes.

"From his speech, I would say he is a gentleman, educated in Philadelphia," Poe ventured. "Where else he lived, I cannot determine from his few words."

"He was a gentleman," Beckwith amended. "And he was born in Philadelphia but spent his youth in the Ohio territory. He is Errol Blennerhesset, the second son of Harman Blennerhesset, the Irish exile who joined Aaron Burr in the treasonable attempt to separate the Louisiana territory from the Union. Although Burr and his father were declared innocent, the son evidently bears the guilt. Unless, of course, he had such a nature that this was to be his fate."

As Beckwith finished this recounting, a husky, middle-aged Negro in a drunken stupor headed directly at him. Poe saw him and tried to draw his companion away. It was too late and the colored man collided with Beckwith and held on to him for support. Beckwith made an attempt to disengage, but the Negro held on. Then the poet noticed that in the grappling the black hands were making their way into Beckwith's coat. This was the trouble he had been warned about and the writer set himself to aid. Then he stopped. The darky was putting something in Beckwith's pocket, not taking anything out! Poe watched as Beckwith pushed him away. Not a word passed between the two men. The Negro swayed toward the entrance and went out. The musicians returned to their crude stand, and the jig started again as the dancers moved to the center of the boards. A few minutes passed as the poet waited for the confidence, but none came.

"It is extremely clever of you," said Poe.

"What is?" responded Beckwith.

"To use a darky as an informer. I saw him pass a message to you. Who would ever think of a Negro as a police agent?"

"We must leave immediately," Beckwith said abruptly.

"What is wrong?" the poet asked.

"If you saw the man there is a chance that others might have done so also. The longer we stay, the greater the danger. In any case, I have gotten what I came for."

When he reached the top of the stairs, the Police Superintendent read the message and returned it to his pocket. They came out of Cow Bay Alley and went down another lane parallel to the Old Brewery, where the mud stuck to their boots. Beckwith had intended to make his way across Paradise Park as the fastest way out of the Five Points. As he glanced backward, he saw movement.

"They are behind us. Run."

Poe had been an excellent runner all his life and always felt exhilaration in outdistancing the pack. He easily passed Beckwith. Perspiration came upon him. The air seemed to turn clear. He remembered that June day in Richmond in his sixteenth year when, as a challenge, he swam seven miles of the James River, from Ludlam's Wharf to Warwick, and then walked home triumphantly. . . . In this reverie he came to an intersection and made a right turn into what he thought was a continuation of the main street. Some yards behind him, he heard the shouting voice.

"No, Poe, no," his companion called. "Come back. You have entered the Abattoir." But Beckwith had caught up to him some twenty-five feet into the dead end. It was too late. A silhouetted line of men blocked their escape.

Beckwith assessed the situation. On both sides of the alley were scabrous tenements, three to five stories high. Then he saw a building with an outside staircase, rickety and uneven. There was only one like it in the Five Points. Beckwith did not know the way, but there was nothing else to do but seek safety inside the maze of the infamous tenement known as Jacob's Ladder.

"This way, Poe. Follow me and do not stop for a moment."

They bounded up. Some of the rotting steps broke as they plunged inside the building. The stench was overpowering. Poe thought he would vomit.

From then it was flight through passages of dirt and vermin and squalor. They burst into a room and nearly upset a seething pot of offal soup cooking on a tiny stove in a space where a Negro couple was sitting on the floor eating a meal from the top of a wooden crate. A toothless old man at the window turned to them, unsurprised at the intrusion. "White men, you're in a heap of trouble," was his quiet appraisal. They went through another room in which there was no furniture, but lying together on a straw mattress were a pretty bare-breasted white woman and a black man with a powerful physique. On and on they scrambled into a hideous panorama of crying children with distended bellies, jumping over drink-sodden bodies, hearing fights between men and men and men and women, seeing boys and girls convulsed in delirium tremens.

They reached the grimy roof and bounded over the dividers of several buildings as far as they could, until they reached a barrier they could not scale. Down a stairwell they went, skipping the missing stairs, banisters collapsing as they hurtled by.

No one seemed to pay attention to their flight. They reached the ground floor. Beckwith tried to find the entrance to an underground passage which would lead them away. Nothing. They could not remain, for their enemies could confine them in an unfamiliar place. There was no choice but to try the street. They moved cautiously along the buildings, but it was a futile effort, for from both sides of the street came men blocking their path. Beckwith and Poe were trapped within the Abattoir.

To Poe it was a skirmish line stretched across the narrow street. In the center was an unshaven bulky man wearing the unkempt uniform of the Five Points, soft felt hat, jacket and trousers, and heavy boots. He had a shillelagh in his hand, with notches cut on either side. The others carried brickbats, iron pipes, and chains wrapped around their fists. In the formation was the little man with the plug hat who had been in the dance room.

"'Tis a lively evening, is it not?" the bulky man sang out. It was a melodious brogue to come from such a brutal mouth, thought Poe.

"That it certainly is," responded Beckwith coolly.

"May I humbly ask, sirs, what your business be in the Five Points?"

"Why, an evening's pleasure, of course."

"And have you found it now?"

"Enough of it to suffice making our leave."

"You hear that, m'lads. These men would be departing. Is it some kind of insult now that you'd be bearing towards us, poor fellas that we be, wanting to depart so soon?"

"None at all. It is as I said. It is an appropriate time to leave."

"Ah, a man who likes to play with words," the bulky man

said, and his tone turned nasty. "You'll be going when I'll be telling you to go. Or maybe you'll not be leaving—ever. First, what be your true business here?"

"I stated it once. It seems you have difficulty with your hearing."

"Just listen to that rude man, will you, lads? My ears are so keen as to hear the lapping of the sweet waters of Killarney Bay even across the great ocean. But if you don't answer directly, you may not have any ears on your head after I've done with you. They'll be tasty morsels for the rats. It's not that I'm doubting your word, you being gentlemen and all that. But Little George here thinks a wee bit differently. Now usually I wouldn't put too much in his saying because he's a Plug Ugly. But seeing that we're right close by, Little George here comes to us. And how can we refuse a brother, especially with nothing better to do this evening? So we thought we'd come and have a look. 'Tis a grand gesture of friendship on our part, even if I am boasting about it m'self, to come from a hot stove and cold cider into a wind blowing to stir the spirits of the Old Sod. Tell me, sirs, what was it that nigger passed on to you back there in Cow Bay? It was more than his whiskey breath and the stink of his clothes. Ah, you're wily ones, you are. Come now, no more fooling. You're policemen, are you not? Tell me so, and I'll let you go. It'll be enough that I guessed right."

"I told you our purpose here."

"I'm sure that you'll be pardoning me for not believing. So have it as you want, m'darlings. We'll come and have a look for ourselves."

He started forward and the line moved with him.

"Stop right there," demanded Beckwith, backing off two steps to where Poe was standing behind him. "Don't come closer or you might be sorry." He took out the Haston. The bulky man guffawed, and obsequious snickers echoed from his gang.

"You think that little gun frightens me? Why, man, there are ten of us here. You'd be struck from this earth before you got two shots off, even if you were lucky enough to hit one of us."

"Then let me enlighten you and see if you care to try it. Both myself and my friend are expert marksmen. My first shot would be aimed at your face. I guarantee that you would be dead by the time you took another step. My second shot would relieve Little George forever of wearing that burdensome hat because he would not have a scalp to place it on. My friend would be less choosy, but would dispose of a few more with his pepperbox. Afterward, this would help our cause." Beckwith snatched the poet's cane and snapped the blade into the open position. "But most of all you had better remember that no matter what happens to us you'd be the first to die."

"'Tis a powerful argument you have there, sir. You're persuasive enough to be an Irishman, but you've not convinced me. What would m'bhoys think? They'd not be wanting a man feared of death for a leader. Still, tonight, with that lovely moon, is not a night for dying either. So like the reasonable men we are we'll come to an agreement. You must open your coats."

"For what purpose?"

"Now, Little George here is not too bright. And in truth neither are some of the other bhoys. Maybe he didn't see what he thought he saw. I'm inclined to m'doubts. The police would never use a nigger. But I can't take any chances, you see. They've been knowing too much about us these days. If you are what you say you are—gentlemen, you'll be dressed like gentlemen. Between that and the money you spent it will be proof enough for me. For no policemen have money to throw around, the likes of which you've tossed about. The city fathers are too stingy to be giving coin to that cause."

He is clever, Poe thought. No wonder he is their leader.

"Agreed," responded Beckwith, "but only you can examine us."

The bulky man walked forward as Beckwith and Poe opened their coats. He scrutinized them.

"Your silent friend is a bit worn, but he has the cut of a

gentleman. 'Tis so, m'buckos, you're gentlemen, you are. And free then to go about the Five Points. And I, Tom O'Gorham, chieftain of the Bowery Bhoys, give m'word on that."

The bulky man turned and his men followed him. Poe drooped with relief. He had started praying for Virginia and Muddie, wondering who would take care of them after he was dead. And then he heard Beckwith speak, and his life disintegrated in the insane dialogue that followed.

"Tom O'Gorham, did I hear you say?" Beckwith articulated. "Is it Tom O'Gorham? Say it."

"The very one. Himself. You've heard of me?"

"Tom O'Gorham, who has not heard of him," proclaimed Beckwith as the bulky man smiled. "Sure'n Mother Machree across the sea has heard of that fat villain," he continued, mimicking a brogue. "Who has not heard of that cowardly thief whom even the scum of the Irish would shun, who picks fights with old men, steals from children, and can only have a woman by putting a knife to her throat."

Poe was confounded. Beckwith had negotiated them out of harm's way and now he was courting the very danger he sought to avoid by baiting the gang leader.

Beckwith continued his harangue. "You can drop the phony brogue, O'Gorham. The closest you've been to Ireland is the wharves. You're the dropping of Patricia Mahoney and Patrick James O'Gorham, and you were spawned in a Cherry Street tenement. You're as Irish as the painted shamrock on the wall of O'Shaughnessy's saloon on Orange Street, where you spend most of your days drinking whatever comes in a bottle. I hope you've been to church for mass lately because your immortal soul is in danger."

O'Gorham's chagrin was replaced by uncontrollable rage. "Heathen," he screamed, "how would the likes of you know so much about my church?"

"Perhaps because I am a Catholic."

"You're too clean to be a Catholic."

"Then I'm God's messenger here to ventilate a foul soul before it enters Hell."

"Hell is where you're going right now, you devil. At 'em, boys, kill 'em," O'Gorham exhorted. He darted in between his men to present less of a target as the gang started forward.

Beckwith fired. The ball hit O'Gorham in the eye and a gel-like substance spurted down along his left nostril. The astonishment that this was happening to him seemed to suspend O'Gorham in midair a few seconds before he fell dead.

The second shot hit Little George. A hole outlined in red appeared in his throat and he continued to gasp as he lay on the street. Poe held his weapon at his side.

"Fire, Poe, fire," urged Beckwith as he was reloading. The rest of the gang came on. Yet the poet did nothing.

"Goddammit, Poe, shoot, shoot!"

Still the writer did nothing as the remaining gangsters came on. Beckwith grabbed the pistol from Poe's hand, firing as he pulled Poe backward. As the tubes of the pepperbox revolved, the bone of the right cheek of one man disappeared, another man's kneecap was blasted away, a third was hit in the side. The distance was short and the men were bunched so Beckwith could not miss. After the fourth man was hit in the groin, the rest turned and scattered.

They were all gone, but Beckwith took no chances. He loaded both weapons. One wounded man began crawling away and another was feigning death but began to reach for his fallen knife. Beckwith stepped heavily on his fingers. He then bent over the fallen body of O'Gorham, turned him over, and said as in a benediction, "Rest in peace, William Dyckman, Abner Simon, Stuart Bradway."

Poe watched. It was as if he were a spectator at an event which did not concern him. When Beckwith pulled out the cartouche box to reload, the piece of paper the Negro had given him fell out and the wind blew it in his direction. Poe picked it up and read the large printing: THE GARROTER IS NOT

HERE. I HAVE NOT SEEN HIM BEFORE. It was a strange message. The first sentence had been written with a steady hand, but the second sentence had obviously been composed hurriedly. The latter words had to be written rapidly, probably just after the black spotted Beckwith in the dance hall. Yet the information was redundant. The first sentence told the whole story. Why would a man in a dangerous situation write unnecessary words? It was illogical, Poe concluded. Therefore, the two sentences pertained to different individuals. Then Poe realized that Beckwith was standing in front of him. The Police Superintendent said nothing but held out his hand. Without a word, Poe returned the paper. In exchange, Beckwith gave him the pepperbox and his cane. As they came out of the Abattoir they saw the Negro who was Beckwith's informant. He was propped against a wall, his head nearly severed from his neck.

9

DECEMBER 1846

NEW YORK CITY
(Lafayette Place)

During the ride back to Lafayette Place, Poe was silent. He awaited an admonishment from Beckwith for his failure to aid when the Bowery Boys attacked. Feeling ashamed, he diverted himself by posing the implications stemming from the incident. What was the meaning of the Negro's second sentence? Was there yet another unnamed suspect in this mystery? Why did Beckwith first conciliate and then deliberately provoke O'Gorham? Did Beckwith have an unstable personality or a perverted sense of humor? The death of O'Gorham was an act of murder, Poe reasoned, since it could have been avoided. Instead of voicing these questions, Poe found himself being asked one.

"I am curious to know, Poe. Why did you not shoot?"

"I have never killed a man, nor do I ever intend to," Poe said.

"I don't understand. You were in the military. You were trained to kill."

"I joined the army to keep from starving. I am a soldier who was never in a battle. In any case, I was with an artillery unit. I could command a gun crew of a bronze six-pounder to drop a round with accuracy at five hundred yards that could kill a dozen men. If necessary, I would do it because it was an impersonal act. I would not see the men I would be destroying."

"Are you telling me that even if your life were in peril you would not defend yourself?"

"I could not say. I have not had to make that decision— when in command of my faculties. So in truth I cannot answer the question."

"What about the Five Points? Would you have let those gangsters kill you without putting up a fight?"

"But they did not kill me, did they? Perhaps I intuitively knew that you would take care of it. So I did nothing. Obviously I was right. If you had not been there, I would not be there."

"Why did you not tell me about this beforehand? I would have been prepared."

"It is not something I would want other men to know. Besides, I did not think that I would have to use the pistol."

"Then you have never killed a man?"

"No."

"Perhaps you should. It might disabuse you of your romance with death, for you have the gift of making death obsessively attractive. I have killed before. It does not suit my disposition."

"But it will suit your reputation," Poe commented dryly.

"Why do you say that?"

"When it becomes known that you killed Tom O'Gorham —particularly under those circumstances—all New York will cele-brate your deed."

"The incident will never be reported. Nor shall you ever relate what happened if you do not wish to void our agreement and forfeit the payment due you."

"I don't understand. You have rid the city of a notorious gang leader, which will bring you the acclaim of every citizen, and you will not acknowledge it."

"I do not wish the renown. That was not my purpose in going to the Five Points. Though meeting O'Gorham was unin-tentional, killing him was not. The deed itself was satisfaction enough. I know that he killed three of my men in the cruelest manner possible. Those were the names I pronounced over his body. I should have added a fourth, but I do not know the name of the old man who was drinking whiskey in a tavern when O'Gorham came over and struck him a blow, crushing his head. 'Why did you do that?' he was asked. 'Well,' O'Gorham replied, 'I was looking at my shillelagh and noticed that there were forty-nine notches, twenty-five on one side and twenty-four on the other; I just wanted to even the sides.' "

"Then you killed in vengeance," Poe said indignantly. "O'Gorham never had a chance. You placed my life in jeopardy for a trivial passion."

"Poe, all passions become trivial in time. I did not know who he was when we first encountered him, but when O'Gorham identified himself, he pronounced his own death sentence."

"But you are a policeman, sworn to uphold the law. When you shot him you made yourself his judge and jury as well as his executioner. And in that act of vengeance you made me an accomplice, nearly forcing me to violate my ethic against killing."

"Precisely, Poe. I will not attempt to deceive you. In a perfect world, where the just reign and the guilty are punished, I would not interfere. Nor would I commit such an act if an iota of uncertainty existed. However, there was no doubt of O'Gorham's guilt. Therefore, I had no compunction in executing him. Let me tell you a story which relates to this, about the first man I killed.

"I spent my boyhood in the town of Utica, where my father owned a store. There was an Indian who occasionally sold pelts to him, an Iroquois warrior who had gone west to follow Tenskwatawa, the Prophet, the half-blind brother of Tecumseh. These two Shawnee brothers had roused the tribes to form a confederacy and begin a religious crusade to purify themselves against the unclean ways of the white man. This was the time of the Second War with England, and their movement received the help of the British. The townspeople hated the old warrior, not only because he was a redman but because many families had had relatives killed in the war. The Indian avoided the town for the most part, but he had come back to live out his days in the forests of his ancestors. He too had lost everyone close to him and was now alone.

"I did not share the feelings of my town, perhaps because my father had lived through the war, perhaps because I felt the Indian fought for a cause he believed in. In any case, I was fourteen when I struck a bargain with him. The Iroquois was to teach me all he knew about the wilderness. In turn, I gave him supplies. He was my tutor, I his partial provider. He was not subservient, I was not superior.

"Over the three years that I knew him he told me about the Confederation of the Six Nations, the Prophet and his purposes, and the death of Tecumseh at the Battle of Tippecanoe. He also confessed his failing to obey the prohibition of his fallen leader, who had forbidden the drinking of liquor. In fact, whenever he got his hands on whiskey he drank himself into a stupor."

Poe became restive.

"In the spring of the third year of our relationship, a store-keeper of the town was murdered. His head was split by an iron-trade tomahawk found lying beside him. A cache of coins he was known to have was gone, as were supplies and whiskey. The Iroquois was immediately suspected and sought. He was found in his hut, wildly drunk. Some of the supplies were there and the whiskey consumed. Sober, there was no more honorable man; inebriated, there was no telling what he would do. I wanted to believe him innocent, but I could not. Not because he was an Indian, but because he was a man who was capable of doing such a deed when drunk.

"The Iroquois was unaware what was happening to him. I pleaded that he be sobered so that they could at least hear his defense. But he was an Indian and he had fought against the Americans. This was to be his belated punishment. The Iroquois was hanged and I did nothing to save him. Indeed, why should I? He was obviously guilty.

"Near the end of that summer, my father was sitting at the

tavern with some of the local merchants. One of them had had too much to drink. He let slip some things about the dead storekeeper. His drunken remarks, coupled with a sudden upturn in his fortune, made all there realize that he was the murderer, not the Iroquois. Ironic, was it not, Poe, that the whiskey which was used as the ingredient for staging a killing should be the selfsame element for unmasking the murderer? My father came home that night in a state of shock. It was almost a duplication of your 'Thou Art the Man.' When I read that story, I could have sworn you knew of that incident in Utica.

"When daylight came and the sheriff went to arrest the real murderer, he had fled. I put on my buckskins and my moccasins and took my long rifle. Taking the trails through the forest that only the Iroquois and myself knew, I pursued this man. I caught up with him two hours later. It was my intention to bring him back. However, at the moment I sighted him I found that I had a fury within me that could not be contained. I became God's avenging messenger. Else why did this all happen? There was no doubt as to his guilt. He had slain one man and was responsible for the death of another. What purpose was there in bringing him back? He saw me and knew why I had come. Perhaps my guilt in failing a friend compelled me to do what I did. I did not give him a chance. What was the point? There was no one in town who could best me. I fired once and he was dead. I was sixteen at the time."

At this point, Beckwith broke off and went into the kitchen. In a while he returned with a pot of coffee. He poured two cups and, handing one to the poet, he continued the recounting.

"The second man I killed was of no consequence. He was an arrogant assemblyman from Chenango County. Envious of my position in Albany, he was as relentless to provoke me as I was to avoid him. He thought because of my age—I was twenty-one at the time—and my disposition, he had an easy victim. He was an offensive man; killing him was a dispassionate act.

"The third man I killed died needlessly. It was an accident

—his, not mine. It also happened in Albany, but three years ago. A young woman of good family fell in love with me. I told her that while she was endearingly beautiful—and she was, Poe—and that I cared for her—and I did—that it was not my purpose to marry at the time. But that only enticed her all the more. She said it was only her desire that I love her. And so I did. I loved her and loved her and loved her, and there was no surcease. Until her father found out.

"He confronted me with the situation, which I did not deny. He accused me of seducing his daughter, which I did deny. I replied that she was a strong-minded young lady who knew her own desires. In fact, strictly speaking, I was the one seduced. He failed to appreciate either the humor or the factuality of that remark. He challenged me to a duel. Of that interview all I could hear was that tedious word *honor:* honor above death, honor above life, honor above fortune, honor even above that supreme quality, good sense.

"He was in his late forties or early fifties. I had no wish to harm him. I offered to resign my post and leave the city. Candidly, there I was being deceitful, Poe, for I was bored with my position, with Albany, and with the young lady. I offered him a high appointive state office. I offered him the assurance of lucrative contracts from the state—provided, of course, he would honestly fulfill them. He refused all these entreaties. There was nothing else to offer except what I would not surrender, my life. So be it, I said.

"At the dueling ground, I asked again that he forsake this nonsense. Still he refused. There was no anger in my heart. I raised my pistol. It was my intention to miss him by shooting close to his side. I reasoned that if I fired in the air he would think I was mocking him and demand another chance, so I brought my shot to his right side. But the foolish man. . . . Perhaps aware of my reputation, for I was now known as someone not to be trifled with, he thought to outwit me and in violation of the code duello stepped sideways as he fired. That maneuver cost him his life. I

111

had no regrets. His obstinacy and lack of honor caused his own death. It would have been easy to cover up the affair, but I was departing from Albany in any case, and I hoped this would deter others from challenging me. It was only with O'Gorham this night that I again felt a fury envelop me as I did just before I avenged the Iroquois."

How he doles out little pieces of himself as if they were cabalistic revelations, Poe thought. Well, at least it is something personal. I have been with this man for some fifteen hours and it has been like being with an automaton. I will know you, Beckwith, whether you want me to or not. I will penetrate the sanctuary of your personality.

"Still," Poe persisted, "I don't understand why you will not take credit for O'Gorham's death."

"Politics," replied Beckwith. "While it is true that the Irish are despised, this is changing. Suppose O'Gorham's death is reported in the manner you suggest. The Irish of the city would not remember that he was a hoodlum and a murderer who robbed and killed even his fellow Irish. He would become a hero who preyed on those who oppress the oppressed. His deeds would be exaggerated by a downtrodden people living in a hostile land who are badly in need of a martyr. He would be romanticized as a Gaelic Robin Hood who was killed by a nativist sheriff. I would be resented by all the Irish, including the honest, the reputable, the hardworking. Summing up, Poe, it would be politically inexpedient to be known as the man who killed O'Gorham."

It was shrewd reasoning, but Poe felt shortchanged. He had hoped to share in the glory of the incident and thus augment his reputation as a writer of action tales.

"Now if I killed an Indian or a Negro, that would be different," Beckwith continued. "Indians and Negroes don't vote. No, we will leave O'Gorham where he belongs, in the streets and to an unsung fate. Before this night is out, his body will be stripped of its clothes and his possessions divided among his compatriots of the Five Points, who will throw his naked corpse into the East

River. It will be fished out at dawn and brought to Dead House. There an enterprising attendant will sell an unclaimed cadaver to a dissecting medical house. And in his end, Thomas O'Gorham may aid humanity by enhancing the knowledge of anatomical medicine.

"And now, Poe, it is very late and I must be in my office in a few hours. It has been enough for one day."

10

DECEMBER 1846

NEW YORK CITY
(Lafayette Place
and Forty-second Street)

Poe awoke with the realization that this was the second consecutive time he had had a dreamless sleep. Perhaps, he reasoned, undergoing actual pathological experiences somehow purged the mind's need to manufacture dreams. Nevertheless, he asked himself which was more excruciating: to experience the groping phantoms incarcerated in his skull or to encounter the live wraiths of the Five Points and the terror of entrapment in the Abattoir?

By the sun's angle he judged it to be about ten o'clock. The poet lay there for a while, absorbing in lambent comfort the bed, the room, the warmth. He heard nothing. Finally he dressed and went into the hall. Still there was no sound. Then he saw the note propped up against a cut-glass vase on the hall table at the head of the stairs.

Poe
The cleaning woman will be in at eleven. She will prepare your meal. The dossiers are in my study across the hall should you wish to peruse them. I shall return at 1 p.m. Please do not leave the house. I have a rigid schedule and should like to maintain it.

Beckwith

Poe turned and went to the room which served as Beckwith's study. There on the desk he saw the folders. He sat down and looked about. Behind him were bookshelves. He could not decipher anything of the man from the eclectic titles. It was as if whoever purchased the books meant them for the sole purpose of filling the shelves. Then he noted the four morocco-bound volumes at eye level near the corner, *The Anatomy of Phrenology: Explanation of an Exact Science.* They seemed too evenly joined. He rose to examine them. Sure enough, the volumes were simply a false front covering the space of about seven inches. He pulled out the bound façade and behind it, built into the solid wall, was a rectangular compartment with a small panel. There did not seem to be any locking device. Poe did not try to open it. He carefully replaced the false book-cover front. Next he tried the desk drawers. They too were locked. Yet despite a raging curiosity, again he did not try entry. Poe intuited that Beckwith would be aware of intrusion no matter how cautious he was. Besides, something so easily opened would not contain anything of worth. (Or could it? He was remembering "The Purloined Letter.")

The writer returned to the chair. If Virginia and Muddie could see me now, he thought, they would know how I appear in a setting more suited to my upbringing. He was not worried about his wife and her mother. They were used to his not returning from the city for two or three days. At least this time they knew where he was! Nor did he concern himself about them. Muddie could handle any situation.

Poe examined the dossiers. While there appeared to be a pattern, there was no hint to the killer as there had been in the murder of Mary Rogers. Her case was relatively simple to follow through the journalistic accounts. From each newspaper he had been able to glean a detail, an angle, a fact which in the refracted light of his analytical power led to the plausible solution. The only effort (and expense) he had put into that case was taking the ferry to the Elysian Fields in Hoboken to examine the area where the woman's strangled body was discovered.

The Garroter killings were elaborately irrational. Even C. August Dupin would be stymied. And shouldn't I know, Poe chortled, since I am Dupin? And if I am that noble French intellectual, then I cast Beckwith as G———, the Paris Prefect of Police who, although of mediocre talents, had the good judgment to request Dupin's assistance.

Beckwith thinks me a romantic. He does not know me as a master mathematician, excellent linguist, superb logician, brilliant analyst, with a profound knowledge of a host of subjects. True, I did write "Sonnet-to-Science," which most people interpreted as a condemnation. It was not a denunciation but a recognition that science—with its callous objectivity—strips the mystery which clothes the world in beauty. No matter how I might despise this, I can discern the future.

If Beckwith were present, I would tell him that mathematics is the language of creation and that poetry is the language of beauty. And that I am aware of the difference.

Beckwith, I would say, here is more proof of my analytical powers. Did I not formulate in "The Murders in the Rue Morgue" a theory of probability, which I further define as the Calculus of Probability in my subsequent story, "The Mystery of Marie Rogêt"? It is a contribution to mathematics yet unrecognized, but I am most proud of it. Yes, if Beckwith were here this is what I would tell him. Or perhaps not. Why should I humble myself?

Sir Richard and Philip Lewissohn, nothing. Madelyn Townshend, dismiss her completely. Paul Motier, I must see him. A common bond, foreigners all. I will recommend to Beckwith that the suspects be placed under observation or that more be found out about their past.

Moran. Perhaps I was hasty in accusing him because of his sexual predilection. And as Poe's hand touched the banker's dossier, the room seemed to grow balmy as if the morning sun were focusing solely on him through the window glass, the air became incredibly vibrant, and there was a heavy hyacinthine scent. It was impossible. He stood up. There were no flowers in the room. In the hall, perhaps. He checked, but there was only the empty vase. He strained to remember. All that flickered into his mind were his own long-ago lines:

> Helen, thy beauty is to me
> Like those Nicean barks of yore,
> That gently, o'er a perfumed sea . . .

Never mind, you know the poem, he chided himself; the line, what is the line?

> Thy hyacinth hair, thy classic face . . .

Had he at last, through some unbeknownst act, broached a finite barrier which bound the human mind, materializing thought? Or was it possible that animal magnetism could be self-induced as well as brought on by an mesmeric operator? Something he had done triggered this phenomenon.

It was as when he would think of a combination of words or thoughts or sounds which so excited him that he was confident he could not ever forget them. Yet when he sat down to write them, the lines eluded him. Sometimes he would strain to recall, but they were ephemeral. And his only remembrance was that he had thought beautiful, elliptical thoughts.

Before Poe could conjecture further, he heard the front door open and went to the stairs to see a stout woman carrying packages. It was Beckwith's cleaning woman, a matronly German. She greeted him with a guttural "Good morning." Evidently she had encountered these situations before; his presence was not questioned. Her only other communication with him was to ask if he cared for anything to eat. When Poe replied that he did, she placed a setting on the dining room table and retired to the kitchen. Some twenty minutes later, Poe had placed before him thickly cut slices of bacon, pieces of steak and veal surrounded by eggs, seeded bread, a mound of butter, and a pot of coffee and another of tea. His appetite was returning, for now the author was able to consume twice the amount of the day before.

Beckwith returned at one o'clock, as Poe expected. Without taking his coat off he asked the poet to accompany him. Poe did not inquire about their destination. He knew that at the appropriate moment he would be informed and given adequate background. He did notice the bulge in his companion's greatcoat pocket. Lord, I hope Beckwith is not carrying a pistol again, he thought. And fear began to edge into him.

As the cab turned onto the Bowery, Poe made his recommendations and the Police Superintendent nodded in agreement. They had gone some distance when Beckwith leaned out of the window and asked the driver to stop.

"Good, they have taken my advice," he said.

"And that was?" asked Poe.

"Putting a fence around Peter Stuyvesant's pear tree," replied Beckwith, pointing to the northeast corner of Thirteenth Street and Third Avenue. "You might be interested. It was planted in 1647. It is the closest thing to immortality we can gaze on."

These last words inflamed the poet. What did this backwoods politician, this unfeeling policeman, know about immortality? I, as a poet and searcher for eternal life, have been seeking it with all my intellectual resources. And Beckwith has the insolence, the arrogance, the ignorance to make this analogy. Poe saw a thick-trunked, hoary tree with only one large limb, from which grew some spare branches. It seemed to be gasping for life. The tree's unwholesome appearance capped the satisfaction of his silent snit.

"In five months it will be two hundred years old," said Beckwith. "It is probably the oldest fruit tree in America."

Poe was still irked by the reference to immortality, more so since he had been forming his next work, his magnum opus. It was to be literally of cosmic proportions. He was developing a theory melding the spiritual with the scientific which would explain the nature of the universe. He would prove the symmetry of matter, that consistency and symmetry were one, that poetry was symmetry and truth was consistency. All was one, one all. Division was death. When total unity was achieved—as it was in the very beginning—death would be vanquished: the conqueror worm would exist no more.

I have attempted, he silently intoned, to pierce the vale of death for the sake of all those lost to me. I have yet to complete my task and Beckwith frivolously couples trees with immortality.

"Why this sudden interest in pear trees, if it has been there for two hundred years?" was the poet's mordant comment.

"It is a propitious omen for the city, which after all was this nation's first capital," Beckwith reminded the writer. "Its health may be symbolic for the future of our country. But to answer your question less metaphysically, all potential historical sites are being appraised. This is not generally known, so I would appreciate it if you were to keep it confidential. New York is to be the site of a World Exposition, probably at mid-century."

"But that is four years from now. It seems a long time to prepare."

"We will need the time, for it is planned to build a massive exhibition hall of iron and glass."

"Similar to the Crystal Palace being built for the London exhibition?"

"Yes, in fact it is to be a replica of that structure. Were it my decision, I would not ape the British but would erect a building indigenous to this New World. However, I have not been consulted in the matter."

"And it will be built in the suburbs, on Sixth Avenue between Forty-first and Forty-second streets, adjacent to the Croton Distribution Reservoir."

"Precisely, Poe. How did you know?"

"If you recall, I mentioned that I often found it necessary to walk home. I have stopped at the reservoir several times. I am continuously amused by its ersatz Egyptian façade and the vulgar taste of the city officials who approved the design. I noted the nearby excavation. It was far too large for an ordinary construction project. I thought it an expansion of the reservoir system. As soon as you spoke of a World Exhibition, I immediately associated the project with it. It is extremely suitable. All other locations in the city would be congested. This is near the city yet would be ample to handle crowds. Also, we are approaching the site now."

The cab had proceeded beyond the Bloomingdale Road, turned onto Sixth Avenue, and was nearing Forty-second Street. The writer had not been there for nine months. When the vehicle stopped and he stepped out, Poe swallowed. There, about a block's distance from the high walls which held the waters of the Croton reservoir, like a sorcerer's hat adorned with mystic symbols enlarged ten-thousand-fold, fantastically high, stood a tower.

"A feat, is it not, Poe?"

"It is a marvel, Beckwith. It appears to be more than three hundred feet high."

"Actually, it is three hundred and fifty feet."

Poe knew he could count on the Police Superintendent for exact statistics. As they walked toward it, Poe mentally calculated that if the tower was 350 feet high, the perimeter of the octagon base was about 140 feet. He noted the structure had fourteen levels, each becoming progressively narrower, until it became almost a point at the top. He estimated each level at 25 feet.

The two men stood at the foot of the tower of timber braced with iron. It was more skeletal at close hand. Poe saw that it was reinforced by diagonal cross-sections. It was the gaps in the uncompleted portions of the X-shaped beams which gave the appearance of huge mystic symbols from a distance. The tower was open on all sides, and there was a staircase straight up the entire length of the structure.

"When completed, there will be an observatory on the fifth and fourteenth levels," Beckwith said. "The center cavity is for the latest technical achievement, a steam elevator which will carry passengers to these lookout platforms."

"Has it been named?"

"Not formally, but the workmen call it Latting's Tower, after Waring Latting, its builder."

Beckwith began climbing the staircase, Poe reluctantly trailing him. He could not contain himself. "Why are we here?"

"I thought you would enjoy a view of the city from an unprecedented height. It should be a magnificent sight. After all, Poe, you are the author of several stories which take place from spectacular points, one even beyond the earth's atmosphere, 'The Balloon-Hoax' and 'The Unparalleled Adventure of One Hans Pfaall' if I recall."

"And 'Mellonta Tauta,'" the writer added.

"Yes, the one set in the future which views earth from a perpetually airborne balloon. It is a clever story."

"Thank you," Poe responded softly, now wary of Beckwith's compliments.

As they climbed higher, it grew progressively colder and the reigning northwest wind was bitter against Poe's face. His eyes began tearing. In sour amusement he thought of a variation of one of his most popular stories. *I should call this "An Ascent into the Maelstrom."*

They had reached the midpoint seventh level when Beckwith paused. It was then that Poe became conscious of harsh beating noises, like multiple horrendous heartbeats. *Perhaps this wood and iron monster is objecting to being trodden upon,* he thought. He looked about, for he had been keeping his head down as a protection against the wind. All about were flags fluttering violently. He felt sure they would rend themselves from their moorings. He recognized the flags of Spain, Portugal, the Austro-Hungarian Empire, and the Kingdom of the Two Sicilies.

"The flags?" Poe fairly shouted.

"It is a test," responded Beckwith, directing his response into the ear of his companion, "as is this structure. The tower was constructed early to see if it will stand; the flags also have been put up prematurely to determine if they can bear the velocity of the winter wind at this height. If they endure, it is planned to fly the flags of all the participating nations each day of the exhibition."

"It will undoubtedly be an inspiring sight," replied Poe, "but will it not be burdensome to remove the flags each dusk and run them up at daylight?"

"Well observed, Poe. You were in the army, and that daily ceremony would be familiar to you. We have received permission from each of the governments and from our Congress to allow the flags to remain permanently on these masts."

Poe was becoming increasingly apprehensive. He had never been this high before, much less on an experimental tower. He feared the powerful wind would sweep him through one of the open sections, and the cold was numbing his toes, fingers, and nose. He pulled up the collar of his guard coat.

"Here, Poe, this will help," said Beckwith. He pulled out a parcel from his left pocket from which he removed a new pair of gloves and scarf.

"But I already have gloves on," said Poe, indicating his cracked black pair. I should have known, he told himself, that Beckwith would be prepared for any occasion. I will resist his charity.

"I brought you here and I am responsible for you," responded Beckwith. "You have no scarf and those are walking gloves, entirely unsuitable for this enterprise." And not to be deterred, Beckwith fitted the new woolen scarf around the poet's neck and gave him the new gloves.

"Very well, but it is a loan," Poe acquiesced. "When we get back down, I will return them." How delightfully warm these gloves are, thought Poe, as he felt the fur lining against his fingers. As Beckwith took his old pair they slipped from his hand and were blown away.

"I am sorry, Poe. That was careless of me. I implore you to keep mine since it was my fault yours were lost."

You do not fool me, Beckwith, thought the poet. You are loose in nothing. Still, he could use new gloves and it would be ungentlemanly to refuse under the circumstances. The warmth of his companion's gesture stayed with Poe until he reached the top of Latting's Tower.

They were on a small platform under the cupola at the highest level. The wind stung Poe's face, and he pulled the scarf across the lower half of his face and pushed his hat down on his head. What kind of demon was this Beckwith that he could conceive these tortures?

"It is worth the climb to see this sight."

It was as close to an emotion as Poe had ever heard from Beckwith. He did as his companion, went to the edge, and braced himself solidly across the chest and above the knees against a diagonal cross-section. He did not look down but straight out.

"Beckwith," he asked, now staring directly into the other's green eyes, "why are we really here? It is not for an esthetic experience, any more than was our jaunt into the Five Points."

"Ah, Poe, I see I cannot hide anything from you. I did come up here for the view, but I also have a theory. We agree that everything the Garroter does is significant, including the physical location of where his two victims were placed. I am now concentrating on this aspect. I have traversed the length of Rivington and Delancey and each thoroughfare between those parallel streets in hopes of finding a connection. I have been unsuccessful. Then I remembered that Latting's Tower could now be scaled. I thought perhaps a new perspective might bring a fresh insight —particularly with you along. That is why we are here."

Poe scolded himself for letting Beckwith get the lead. That is what I should have been doing instead of sleeping and eating.

Braced as he was against the cross-section, Poe felt the vibrations of a tower made queasy by the buffeting wind. Then his absurd thought was to applaud the courage of his fictional characters whose compulsions forced them to leave the earth's surface, for now he fully appreciated the dangers to which he had exposed them.

Just above him were rotund white clouds moving in uneven formations. Poe had a desire to reach up and capture a cloud. Instead, he turned in the direction of the impotent sun in the rich blue sky. Only then did he have the resolution to look down. He was viewing the city as through a stereoscope, his eyes shifting from depth to flatness to depth. He gazed from the shoreline of the far side of the East River on his left to the high point of Brooklyn Heights directly ahead to the sheer outcroppings of the Palisades of New Jersey on his right.

Manhattan was an island tilted to the sea. It was laid siege to by a motley fleet. Ships of every type congested its waterways except at the very tip, where from Battery Park the circular Castle Garden jutted offshore. There were transoceanic clippers, double-masted schooners, steamers with sails, intracoastal paddlewheel steamers, the cross-city steam ferries, and a host of smaller boats. Poe could not begin to count the number, nor could he see a single available berth.

Directly below were the half-frozen waters of the Croton reservoir. Farther on, amid the majestic landscaping of Union Place, were sumptuous mansions. The grid pattern of the streets made it possible to look far down the town to Washington Square. He saw a tree-lined Fifth Avenue, the tall white steeple of Grace Church at Broadway and Tenth Street, and on the Bowery the equally high spire of St. Mark's Church. His eyes reached to City Hall Park, and he could outline the steeples of the North Dutch Church at Fulton and William streets and the Middle Dutch Church at Nassau and Liberty. He was able to identify the Brick Church's spire by a direct alignment with the City Hall tower. From above, it was a metropolis of spars and steam and sails and steeples. Yet the only motion was the arrested pace of tiny ships and tinier vehicles.

As he turned slowly in the opposite direction toward West-chester County, he could make out the shoreline settlements at Turtle Bay and Kip's Bay, the villages of West Farms and Ford-ham, and, at wide intervals, suburban villas and farmhouses. And everywhere, winter-barren fields and trees. The Hudson River sloped over the horizon in a laced line. The forests dominated, soiled only by roads. From this height, to the poet, it was a tranquil world, soothing and unpeopled.

The Police Superintendent was raptly studying the lower eastern side of Manhattan.

"Can you see anything, Poe?"

"I see nothing, Beckwith."

They descended, and Poe felt as if he had entered a tropical clime. He quickly removed his gloves and scarf. The climb had been as fruitless as the trip to the Five Points, as far as he was concerned. He was now determined to strike off on his own. "With your permission, I would like to pursue some ideas not worth the bother of both of us," he lied.

Beckwith had more planned, but it could wait. Perhaps a respite was the best thing at this point. "Of course. If you need me, leave word with any policeman." He did not know how to say it tactfully, but he used a gentle tone, calling after the writer, "Poe, do not get into any difficulty, and please do not drink."

The only response he got was the wave of a raised hand as the poet walked off, the early afternoon sun reflecting unkindly on his threadbare back.

11

DECEMBER 1846

NEW YORK CITY
(Chatham Street, Lafayette Place, Rector Street, and Tenth Street)

"I have examined her and there is nothing I can do," pronounced Dr. Walter Reich. He was sitting opposite the Police Superintendent, his immaculate hands cupped over his cane, his spare frame leaning forward.

Beckwith had returned to his office. By late afternoon, he had finished the routine business and was studying the city maps when his visitor came.

"Mrs. Poe is in the terminal stage of consumption. Nothing will cure her now."

"And her present condition?"

"She will have brief periods of invigoration, but these will be euphoric. Then probably a sudden and final collapse."

"And your prognosis?"

"Mrs. Poe will die within a year of a severe hemorrhaging of the lungs."

Damn, thought Beckwith, that it could happen to that pretty, innocent child (he could not think of Virginia as a woman). Damn too that if it happens soon it will distract Poe and disrupt my schedule.

"Then there is nothing more to be done."

"The only thing is to make her as comfortable as possible,"

Dr. Reich said. "I prescribed medicine and am having it delivered with the food which will best nourish her. It has been billed in your name, as you instructed."

"I thank you for all you have done, especially since it took you so far from the city," Beckwith said.

"Not at all, Superintendent. It was my pleasure. I have been waiting to return your favors. Our faculty is most grateful for the protection of the police and the cooperation of the authorities at Dead House. Your enlightened attitude has done much to advance our work. We have come a long way in this city from the days of the Doctor's Riots, when it was necessary to dissect the human body in secret for fear of being dismembered by the mob. In this connection, I have been authorized to ask if you would care to become a member of the Board of Trustees of the Columbia College of Medicine."

"I am greatly honored, sir. May I think about it?"

"Of course." The physician rose to leave.

"Dr. Reich," said Beckwith abruptly, as if he suddenly formed the question, "does the number thirteen have any significance in the Hebrew faith?"

"Yes, it does," the physician replied, taken aback by the radical change in topics. "In the thirteenth year the male is considered man-grown and there is a ceremony called bar mitzvah. It formalizes his acceptance into the religious community."

"Would it be accurate to characterize it as a rite of virility?"

"Technically, it would be correct if one compares it to other cultures. Particularly, if the sentiment of the day, 'Today I am a man,' is accepted at face value. However, it would be an extreme statement if one equates bar mitzvah with virility or physical prowess, either medically or semantically. The ability of the Jewish boy to master passages of religious tract and to demonstrate this proficiency to his elders could hardly be considered a virile act. Is there some particular reason you ask this question?"

"Not really. It is an incidental point I wanted some further information about."

"There is one more aspect. There is within Judaism an obscure sect called Cabalists. They believe in an occult theosophy or mystical interpretation of the Scriptures. For them the holy books hold a hidden meaning of divine revelation which can be obtained through deciphering letters or numbers. The Cabalists, who included a few Christians in their early history, have been the source of much magic and demonology, from the medieval period to this day. I do not know what the number thirteen signifies to them, but I can find out for you."

"It is a kind offer, but really unnecessary. I know Rabbi Gomez of the Spanish-Portuguese synagogue. This will give me an excuse to visit him."

"Superintendent, is this something which concerns the Jewish community?"

"Not at all, Dr. Reich, merely curiosity on my part," reassured Beckwith. There was no point in causing alarm on a potentiality. "By the way, I have decided to accept your trusteeship, but on one condition."

"And that is?"

"That you informally poll the board to be certain that I will be accepted when my name is submitted."

The doctor paused a moment and then smiled as he left.

Beckwith wished he too could smile. He was saddened to learn of Virginia Poe's condition. He was greatly tired and a little discouraged. Not implementing the next stage of his plan this night suited him. It was now past five o'clock and he decided he had done enough. He would work on his correspondence at home and retire early.

Perhaps it was his blighted mood, but he walked home in a brooding darkness more like midnight than dusk. It was quiet as he entered Lafayette Place. The only sounds were caused by the hooves of a horse on the cobblestones and the footfalls of pedestrians. The iron gate creaked as he opened it. He loosened his greatcoat and reached into his jacket pocket for the key. He was bending slightly to reach the latch when he heard the click.

Beckwith knew exactly what it was. He whirled, too late. The point of a sword cane was at his chest. It was being held by a gray glove which blended into a gray sleeve protruding from the deep shadow near the Corinthian column.

I cannot, I will not be taken this way, was his instantaneous thought. Swiftly Beckwith dropped to the ground and rolled to his left. He came to rest facing upward, intending to spring to his feet. But the disembodied hand had a cunning of its own. It followed the ploy. This time the blade was at his throat.

———

At that moment, Poe was emerging from Count Motier's rooms in a boardinghouse on Rector Street. It had been a satisfying visit only in the sense that he had been able to converse in French, something he had not done for a long time.

Poe posed as Beckwith's surrogate. He pretended that his companion was seeking honorable means to avoid a duel. The writer probed, but he could not detect a flaw in the young noble's background.

Motier continued to be offensively cocky and lacking in civility. Most objectionable to Poe was that he was offered no refreshments. Nevertheless, there was nothing to contradict Motier's claim that he was the nephew of the great Lafayette. The only untoward item Poe noted was that Motier seemed to be going on a journey. Although the Frenchman was in his dressing gown during the interview, laid out on the bed in the next room were clothes, boots, and a carpetbag. It was rather late in the evening to begin the travel that these accouterments suggested, Poe thought. The poet left the boardinghouse in the direction of Morris Street, then changed his mind and turned toward Lumber Street, the direction from which he had come. Yes, the same man was standing in the entrance of a closed store. There was no doubt about it. Beckwith's man was watching Motier.

So much for this, Poe thought. Now for my next project, investigating the investigator. He felt guilt at this undertaking, especially since it was diverting him from finding the Garroter.

However, he wanted to know more about his patron. It irked him that the Police Superintendent, a provincial, was a rival. He was supposed to provide the superior mentality. Poe recognized his own envy: Beckwith's acumen was disconcerting.

———

"Do you surrender, Police Superintendent?"

"Have I a choice?"

"Not really."

"Then I leave the decision to you."

The tone was decisive, the voice husky. Beckwith had heard it before, but where? There was soft laughter.

"Spoken like a politician. When overcome by a reality do not make a commitment but rather a compromise."

"Concession is the lifeblood of politics."

"Then be grateful I am not a politician, for if I were, with you in that position, you would have no lifeblood left."

The blade withdrew and a figure completely in gray stepped into the vaporous blue light. Yes, he decided, it would have been difficult to tell otherwise in those clothes, but he would have known by the long eyelashes. The gray figure snapped the blade in place and turned the cane around, holding the head toward Beckwith to help him to his feet.

He found himself looking at the carved figure of the Greek goddess Diana. "No, thank you," he muttered. "I have had enough of that cane for one evening." He got up and opened the front door. "Please come in, Lady Townshend."

"As a passionate democrat, I felt sure you would address me as Mrs. Townshend."

"You play a dangerous game, ma'am."

"Better than no game at all."

"I am quite serious. Either one of us could have been injured needlessly."

"A game without consequence is not very interesting."

"Lady Townshend, this is not the stage of the Drury Lane or the court; this straining for repartee is tedious."

"You are, of course, speaking for yourself."

"I always do."

Beckwith was hardly enthralled to see the Englishwoman. He did not like surprises. Moreover, she had dispensed with her femininity and was capable of managing without it. He was unsure of how to cope with her. He decided to be as blunt as she was.

"Why do you wear men's clothing, like George Sand?"

"It allows me freedom of movement, literally and figuratively. Crinolines are confining and convention more so. Why should I be caged at night, like some animal in a zoo, because I am female? In fact, it was George Sand who gave me the idea."

"But she wields a pen, not a sword cane."

"She finds her pleasure one way and I in another."

He helped her off with the greatcoat, watching as her fingers glided unself-consciously to her throat, discarding the cravat and opening the buttons of her shirt until the cut of her breasts showed.

"Drury Lane, George Sand. You are quite the cosmopolite, Mr. Beckwith."

"I read a good deal."

Her presence was simultaneously annoying and pleasing. After all, how many women would have her audacity? Careful, Beckwith, he told himself. She is not only another man's wife but a suspect. But the game is interesting, so let us continue.

"My apologies, Mr. Beckwith."

"For what, ma'am?"

"For using the sword cane. It was inexcusably foolish. I have never done such a thing before. Let me explain. My father was in the diplomatic service and I have been a resident of many countries. For my protection, I was permitted to learn defensive arts. Add to this my restless nature as well as my curiosity. With this background, it is intolerable for me to languish at home when I am in the most exciting city in the New World. But for a woman to wander alone at night would make me vulnerable to all types of unpleasant situations. To obviate this, I wear men's clothes and carry this stick for protection. Waiting for you for more than an hour made me restless. When you did finally arrive, for some inexplicable reason I did that stupid thing. I suppose it was because I was told I was skilled with the sword cane and wanted to try it with an able opponent. It was really a mad impulse."

From a decanter on the sideboard, he poured her a brandy. Whatever else, he now knew who the gray stranger of the police reports was. Her story sounded plausible. Still . . .

"Lady Townshend, why are you here?"

"My boots are pinching. Please, Mr. Beckwith, I would be more comfortable without them."

She sat down near the fireplace and held one foot out. He approached cautiously, so as not to be surprised if the point of her toe were to swing to his chin. He faced her, and with his pulling motion she became more horizontal. The curves of her breasts could not be hidden within the shirt. A wayward glance went to the rounded area above her crotch. He was close enough to see slight lines around her eyes. He told himself she was no longer young, but as much as he tried he could not stem desire. I will not allow myself, I will not become involved—even if the opportunity presents itself, he steadfastly admonished himself.

"Lady Townshend, why are you here?" he repeated.

"I bring a message—from Sir Robert Peel. He says, 'The arrangement is still in effect and the vista expanded.' She reached up and the tightly coiled light brown hair was undone. It unfurled to her shoulders.

"You are tardy, ma'am," he replied, not trying to disguise his irritation. "I have been aware of that for the past eight months."

"You put me in a most unusual position, Mr. Beckwith. I am not used to apologizing once, much less twice, in one evening. An explanation is in order.

"While I was in the Queen's retinue it was my good fortune to become acquainted with Sir Robert. He is a capable and dedicated man, a bloody relief from most others in the government.

I was helpful to him on several occasions. We became friends. When he learned that I was coming to America, he suggested, among other recommendations, that I should seek out a Hollis Beckwith and convey this message as a favor. And that was my intention soon after I arrived on these shores.

"And now I will be unflattering, Mr. Beckwith. After I came to this city I made inquiry to find you. Many knew your name by your position, but little else. You seemed to be a man without substance. It was said that you were influential, but to what extent no one knew. It was said that you were ambitious, but what your goal was no one knew. It was said that you were a man of power, but no one could discover its base. It was said that you were a man of enormous wealth, but no one could assess its extent or source. You were labeled a cruel and cold man, but no one could cite examples. I thought that such an ambiguous man must have an ambiguous personality. I had no desire to meet you. If it should happen that we met I would give you Sir Robert's message and my obligation would be ended. After all, he did not attach any urgency to this errand. Thus it was until we met in Mr. Schuyler's home. How do you come to know Sir Robert?" The boots were off and she sipped the brandy.

"It is really a simple story. I was offered the assignment as Police Superintendent two years ago. It was an innovative position. There was only one other man who had done it before and, from my reports, done it quite well. So I wrote to England and requested his counsel. Sir Robert was gracious enough to give me his fullest advice in this matter."

"Then you have never met him?"

"I only know him through our correspondence. And your relationship with him?"

"As I said, I moved in the Queen's circle. Sir Robert would flatter me by asking my reactions to legislation pending in the Parliament and other matters, and my opinions on certain personages privy to Her Majesty."

"Then you were in his employ?"

"What Sir Robert asked, I answered in candor, as I would

for anyone who posed similar questions. What I observed I repeated as I would to any friend in a conversation. In fact, I am not sympathetic to his Tory faction in Parliament, but I admire the man. And I assure you nothing profound took place in British government because of any impression or information I conveyed to Sir Robert. And the message I brought you. What is its significance?"

"Since Sir Robert evidently thought you are trustworthy enough to bring the message, you are trustworthy enough to know the answer. It simply means that the information we transmit to each other will be expanded to other than police matters."

"You are an ardent Democrat, both in party and political philosophy. Why do you deal with Sir Robert, an English Tory?"

"Before all other things, ma'am, I am an American. However, love of my country does not blind me to other useful purposes which may be facilitated by friendship with a powerful British official. Though I am not in the national government myself, I am in a position to convey information so that it does the most good."

"But the relations between our two nations have hardly been cordial over the years. What if the information you desire touches a sensitive area?"

"Sir Robert and I have an agreement not to request such information. If our need should inadvertently touch on national security, we ignore the subject."

"But the very avoidance of an answer would signal to the other that a sensitive matter is taking place."

Beckwith searched her face. She picks up too fast, he thought. "Let me put it this way, Lady Townshend. I know Sir Robert's policies. Through the years he has never deviated from promoting stable relations between America and England, and he has proven it by assiduously pursuing that policy in or out of power. Frankly, I am not an admirer of the British, but I support the policy of peace. I believe that these United States would be better off isolated, uncontaminated by Europe."

"Truly amazing. Sir Robert must be as awed at finding a rational American as you must be at finding a capable British noble."

"Now, Lady Townshend, discounting the transmission of an outdated message, I would still like to know the reason for your presence here besides testing your skill with the blade."

"I will answer, but first I am in need. Is there . . . upstairs?"

"Yes, in the guest bedroom."

"Come, do show me the way. Besides, I am used to prime facilities. Which is your room?" At the staircase, Beckwith allowed her to walk ahead. Her man's shirt had worked its way out of her trousers. He had an impulse to place his hands on her hip and feel the undulating movement as she walked up the stairs. But the longing in him would not have stopped there, not stopped there. . . .

"In here, Lady Townshend. I will wait downstairs."

"Nonsense, talk to me. I will not be long and I do not like to waste time." And she went into the bathroom, leaving the door a quarter open.

"To repeat the question," said Beckwith, determined not to be distracted, even by his own aroused desire. "Why did you come here tonight?"

Poe was furious. This was the sixth newspaper office he had been in and he had found next to nothing about Beckwith in the back issues. All the stories had the same monotonous theme as the article he was now looking at.

POLICE SUPERINTENDENT
APPOINTMENT CONFIRMED,
ANNOUNCEMENT SPARKS
POLITICAL CONTROVERSY

Whigs Accuse Democrats of
Abridging Freemen's Liberties,
Tyranny Held Inevitable

Office Labeled Foul Import
A Device to "Englishize"
This Country's Glorious Institutions

Native Americans in Favor,
Will Restore Law and Order,
Preserve God's Holy Sabbath

Albany Politician Selected,
Lack of Experience by Candidate
For Chief City Policeman Cited

In the verbiage of conflicting views and supporting opinions was
the only biographical reference to the new municipal official:

> The Honorable Mr. Hollis Beck-
> with held an important administra-
> tive position within the executive
> council of the New York Democratic
> Party in our State Capital for the past
> several years.

It was frustrating. Poe had used up half the evening with
little gain. His throat was dry. He needed a drink. No, not yet.
He knew even a drop would ruin his present good fortune. Lauda-
num would do for the next few days.

He would query his journalist acquaintances along Nassau
Street. Perhaps they knew something. Also, he had an idea how
the Garroter transported his victims. In the morning he would
check its validity. Poe thought of returning to the comfort of
Beckwith's house but quickly dismissed it as an uninteresting
place to spend the night.

———

There was no shyness in the husky voice beyond the door.
Rather, Beckwith was slightly embarrassed. He had never held a
conversation with a woman who was in the bathroom.

"When we were asked to Mr. Schuyler's home, it was my
intention to refuse," she called through the slightly open door.
"After all, it would be impolitic to involve the British envoy-

136

general in a murder investigation. It would have been easy to stay away because of his diplomatic immunity. But my husband is a kind man. He insisted that it was our duty to help.

"I was still disinclined to go until I learned that you and Mr. Poe would be present. At last, I would be able to fulfill my obligation to Sir Robert and also meet America's most notorious poet. You may not be aware of this, but your friend is becoming known among the English literati through his correspondence with Elizabeth Barrett Browning. It is said that it is not so much that she admires his poetry, but rather that she is fascinated by his macabre topics."

"It is the reverse in France," Beckwith interjected. "An influential critic named Baudelaire appraises his work as genius."

"I was most anxious to meet Mr. Poe. I heard that besides his talent he has magnetic eyes and satanic good looks, and that when he reads his love poems the ladies fairly swoon. Of course, other unflattering things were said about our Raven man, but that only stimulated me. And so I did meet Mr. Poe yesterday and was disappointed."

"Why?" Beckwith called across the room.

"Because you were there," she replied as the door opened.

At the sight of her his breath stopped momentarily, his senses scrambled. Beckwith did not know what the devil to think. If it were a print, the apparition before him could be ludicrously captioned "Aphrodite in Underwear" or "A Modern-Day Astarte." However, the last thing he felt was levity.

The Lady Townshend who stood before him was lucid sexuality. Her lips were slightly reddened, her lashes darkened, her long hair neatly brushed and curled up at the end. She had discarded her trousers. The tight underwear stressed her form, from the inward waist to the rounded hips to the tapering legs.

"When I saw you there, how you carried yourself, what you did and how you did it, there was such stirring in me. Hollis, have you been told that there is in you a masculinity that overwhelms a woman? No, I can see from your blush that you never have. You have the quality nevertheless. Perhaps women have been too shy to tell you; perhaps they could not define the feeling themselves. Many women would be frightened by someone like you. There is also a coolness to you, but that augments your attractiveness. You have the virile quality of which every woman dreams."

Beckwith remained silent, not necessarily believing her but enjoying what she was saying. He rose and moved toward her. The Englishwoman was voluptuous and intelligent. Hell, strike the last word. What did he care about her intelligence? She was lovely. On the other hand—he could not stop his calculating mind—she was trouble from every aspect. Then Beckwith decided. If he were younger he would have been resolute; he would have had the self-discipline to resist. However, he was thirty-five. He probably would never again meet a woman like her, ever.

"Do or say something," she demanded, "or I will put on my trousers and go home."

Beckwith put his hands under her shirt so he could feel bareness as he kissed her. This was the last test to assure himself that what was happening was not some kind of joke and that at the last second there would be ridicule. Her response was the warranty he needed.

He opened the buttons of her shirt, and she held up her arms as he pulled it over her head. Then from the waist he pulled down her underwear. She held onto his shoulders as she stepped out of the garment. He appreciated each of her movements. As she stood nakedly beautiful before him, she asked, "Now would you please call me Madelyn?"

———

Poe stood in front of the house of his dear Loui at 51 Tenth Street. It was getting late. He was debating whether to go in. She might not be alone, and he wanted her all to himself this night. If he sought male company, he was likely to succumb to convivial temptations. With Loui, he was safe. She understood him; in fact, she understood him too well.

Mrs. Marie Louise Shew was the widow of a merchant, of whom she never spoke, and the daughter of a physician, with whom she now lived. She had met Poe at a private reading in the home of a friend. A woman of discernment, she recognized him as a great talent. The poet, mistaking her interest for infatuation, and himself attracted to her—for at thirty-one she was fetching —flirted shamelessly with her. After being romantically rebuffed, he found she had an incisive sense of criticism. Also, Loui never wanted anything from him except that he continue his work. She was always a comfort.

Nevertheless, every so often Poe would become impetuous and play at being the lover. Mrs. Shew took it all in stride; she knew that he did the same things with other women, usually aspiring poetesses.

Poe's problem was that he was attracted to aware females who could plumb his personality. Their rejection of him usually led to rash actions on his part which compromised their reputation. However, the year before, Poe was so often in Mrs. Shew's company that scandalous stories reached Fordham village. Poe had dallied before, but the persistence of the rumors alarmed Mrs. Clemm. Virginia also heard these distortions, but she never doubted that her Eddie was faithful. She cherished her cousin-husband, and never in their eleven years of marriage did she question him about another woman. After all, she had fallen in love with him; was it not natural that other women did? Aware that she lacked the intellectual depth to interest her husband, Virginia encouraged his cerebral friendships with other women.

To quash these calumnies, Mrs. Shew decided to meet his family. It was one of the best things that ever happened to the Poe household. When she saw their poverty-stricken state, she immediately solicited funds, raising some $60. The blankets and nightgowns which warmed Virginia came from her home. When Poe became critically ill, she traveled to Fordham every other day to care for the writer and his sickly wife. As the daughter of a doctor, she had absorbed considerable medical knowledge and was an efficacious nurse. Both Mrs. Clemm and Virginia grew to love their Loui.

Poe moved toward the front door. He sorely needed succor. He knew that he would be asked to stay the night. It was perfectly respectable; her father would be the chaperone. It would be a pleasant evening. He would read amorous poetry to his dear Loui, and perhaps in her kindness she would allow him to hold her hand.

———

There was a fullness to her: her presence, her form, her emotions. Beckwith was concentrating on the looks of her. She had a body which had reached maturation. It was at the apex of perfection, never having been thus and never again to be thus. He felt fortunate that she had chosen him to love her at that moment.

It was so precious that he wanted it to be indelible. He did not, however, trust his eyes to retain the memory. So he shut them and like a blind man ran the edges of his fingers slowly through the long hair, gently over her face, momentarily pausing at her closed eyelids, her nostrils, and her slightly parted lips. Then his fingers ranged in a wider area. Slowly, gently, over her breasts and nipples, curving in and under the wideness of her belly, gliding down in overlapping motions, touching over and over again until he reached the opening between her legs; then, with the four long fingers eased just inside her vagina, continuing the gentle motion.

He eased her over, and the fingers caressed the back of her neck while his face settled in her hair. Then across the slight slopes of her back across from side to side his fingers went, from the small of her back into the crevice of her behind, up and back again and again with the four longer fingers till he felt moisture. Then his hand moved from the bottom of her left leg in a sweep across her thighs to her vagina to the sole of her right foot.

In the swirls of his fingertips would be stippled the memory. All he needed to do when he wanted to remember was to touch the tips of his fingers together.

Still, it was not enough for him. Venus was a myth, Astarte was a legend, Aphrodite was an ideal. But here and now they were all his, and perhaps never again. He would take no chance. His mouth would be another testimonial. He wanted the taste of her, so that when he next spoke of love the sounds formed by his tongue and the words shaped by his lips would be witnesses to this memorial.

He stretched full length beside her and laid his hands on the lustrous hair and kissed her on the mouth. Then, sliding slowly downward, he kissed her throat, pausing to feel the pulse with his lips. Next his tongue lingered at her breasts and nipples. Then he went to the inside of her thighs, leaving a streak of slight moisture as an outline. He eased within her open legs and held her tightly. And, as if nature had endowed him with the gift of deliquescence, for a long, long time he mouthed her.

Madelyn was passive until that moment. Now, without speaking, she indicated that she wanted him to enter her. He mounted and felt the parting. He was bound in sensuous containment. If it ended here, at this moment, he would have been satisfied. And for him that is where it usually ended.

Beckwith had a monstrous ego, as he analyzed himself. That shortcoming was amplified because he kept his vanity to himself. He set the highest criteria for himself in all matters and was discontent unless he fulfilled them—no matter how he was praised by others. He was that way when he made love. It was his objective that his partner be pleased no matter how much it might detract from his own pleasure. He could never lose himself in unfettered desire; he always had to make sure his lover had her orgasm. He had mastered coitus interruptus. This accomplished two purposes: It assured the woman her climax without worry about being impregnated; it also obviated paternity. Love could fade but a pregnancy could not. Thus in the utter gratification of his lovers was reflected Beckwith's pride.

Beckwith was circumspect in all his movements. He put no undue weight on her. He watched as Madelyn moved in rhythm with him, kissing her lips but not too long. He wanted to hear the uncontrollable sighs of her climax.

She was nearing her ecstasy, and he felt the surge also. For a moment he gave pause to the thought that he would stay in her. He dismissed it. He did not know enough about her. Suppose she became pregnant. A moment more. . . . He felt the frenzy in her, and so intense was her feeling he was aware of the sounds forming in her body before she uttered them. A second more and he would withdraw. And then she came, and in an instant so would he. It was time now, move off. As he tried, he felt her arms, which had been around his neck, move farther down his back and her legs entwine with his and hold him tight. He resisted. Her strength was no surprise, but the movement was. She locked him in. And he came into her, into the very marrow of her body.

Later, she lay against a pillow and he brought her cognac. As he held it, Madelyn kissed him for a long time.

"And that was for?" he asked.

"Being a considerate lover." Then after a pause she said, "Would it hurt your ego if I made a comment?"

"By asking the question you have already hurt my ego. So go ahead."

"You are kind and thoughtful. A woman could love you for these qualities alone. And you are good, but you lack spontaneity. You are, in your lovemaking, as you are undoubtedly in your work, proficient. I'm sorry. I hope I haven't hurt you. It was as when I first saw you and knew I wanted you. I thought in my own vanity, I will change those cool jade eyes. But I have not, have I? Perhaps the fault is mine. I am incapable of breaching that reserve of yours. That does not make you less than you are, but by your inability to lose yourself, you deprive yourself. I'm sorry. I did enjoy it so, but I want it to be better for your sake. I feel selfish."

Beckwith did not respond. He never argued with the truth. Instead, he countered with, "Now I would like to ask, Why did you do what you did, force me to stay inside you?"

She looked at him and then to his astonishment this self-possessed woman began to cry. The tears started welling. Then she sobbed convulsively. Beckwith was momentarily stunned, but he knew that females cry at the most unlikely times and for inexplicable reasons.

He held her to console her, and some black running off her lashes was pressed into his chest. He said nothing. He had learned long ago that in these situations it was unnecessary. Wait long enough and a woman will invariably tell. Madelyn dried her eyes against the sheet.

"I wanted you in me. I wanted it all. You need not worry about my becoming pregnant. I am barren."

That answered that, but he understood only part of it. He waited. The answer would come.

"I cannot conceive. I am unfulfilled. God has not made me a complete woman."

Not complete from your viewpoint, and perhaps not from God's, but certainly complete from mine, Beckwith thought. He did not say it aloud, even if it was a compliment. It was not a matter for jest. Why she was so anxious to have a child he did not know. Parenthood never seemed to him a particularly desirable state.

So this is why virility is important to her. It also explains her connection to Harrison Carpentar. The stud role. Beckwith was about to be unhappy. Still, he thought, if I am being used, it is a pleasant way to be used.

"How can you be sure it is you? Modern medicine is proving that the deficiency is not always with the female."

"Sir Richard is not my first husband. I was nineteen and virginal when I was married in St. Petersburg. He was an Austrian military attaché. We were very much in love. We wanted a child, but after a year nothing happened. I went to a doctor. He said I could never conceive."

"Did you ask why?"

"No. That was all I had to hear. What does it matter why?

Two months later, my husband was killed. A defective cannon exploded while he was watching Russian army maneuvers. He was torn to pieces by the shrapnel. I was a widow at twenty.

"I tried with other men, hoping that it was not me. None had the power to requite my emptiness."

"Then not even Harrison Carpentar was able to help?"

"Oh, my God," she exclaimed teasingly, "is it possible that I have not been the only one penetrated tonight? Do I detect jealousy? I am flattered. But listen to me, Hollis Beckwith, and listen carefully. Then judge and do what you will.

"It is not necessary for me to love you or for you to love me. I am not an ingenue and do not expect it. My marriage was kept secret for my father's sake. It would have damaged his career for his daughter to marry a Catholic. However, I did retain my self-respect. I have had lovers, but always, when I chose, it was with the thought that the man had the power to impregnate me. With this hope, I asked myself, Would I want him to be the father of my child? Carpentar is magnificently proportioned, but an oaf in every way. Do you think, if he were my lover, it would be bruited about? If Sir Richard suspected, Carpentar would be a dead man. I have told my husband of Carpentar's attentions, and he knows them to be innocuous. If I wanted a man just for his looks, it would have been Poe. He is a bit short, but he has fine, dark eyes. I also admire intellect. And he is a sensitive man."

"Yet . . . ?"

"He is a romantic. Worse, a romantic poet. When it comes to women, poets are liars and romantic poets are the worst liars. I do not recognize any of his women. They do not exist except in his febrile imagination. He would make me over into one of his brunette creatures of decay and death. I am life seeking after life."

"Your husband, how much does he know?"

"After I returned to England, I vowed I would not marry. Then Queen Victoria ordered my match with Richard Townshend. I suppose she thought she was rewarding me. I was approaching the age of spinsterhood and did not have a dowry. I resisted. However, one does not oppose the wishes of Her Majesty. There was even a hint that my father's pension would be cut off.

"Finally, to break this arrangement, I told Sir Richard of my barrenness. He responded that he had been a soldier all his life and was used to taking orders. Since the marriage had been requested by the Queen, as a loyal subject he would not disobey. He was very gallant. He said he thought me an adornment. He appreciated my truthfulness, said that he was disappointed, of course, but that the matter need never again be discussed. He was equally frank. He said that he was ambitious and that he needed Victoria's favor to advance. I never told him of my first marriage. To what point? If my infertility could not discourage him, nothing would." Madelyn began crying again.

This was not the first time Beckwith had been the confidant of a woman. It always amazed him that women would relate to him, almost a stranger, without the slightest urging on his part, the most intimate details of their lives.

Evidently Sir Richard did not have the particular wherewithal to correct Madelyn's deficiency. Beckwith doubted that he did either. But he did assuredly have the enthusiasm to try. In another respect, he might have the cure. He would make discreet inquiries at the Columbia School of Medicine.

"Does your husband know about your nocturnal escapades?"

"No. His work takes him away for days at a time. Besides New York, he has been charged with inspecting the subordinate consuls in Boston and Philadelphia. He also travels to Washington to confer with the ambassador. That was one reason I decided to undertake these adventures. I am alone for days at a time."

"And this is one of the occasions when he is gone?"

"Yes."

"And your servants?"

"There is no difficulty. I slip in and out of the house. I do not think they suspect anything. And I never entertain alone at home."

Beckwith was delighted. Whatever else was to be, she would stay with him this night.

"Are you positive your husband does not know?"

"I am. He disregards my sterility, but he would never be dishonored. Nevertheless, I pursue my own remedy. I warned him not to marry me. I bear great guilt for his sake. I pray for his forgiveness and do all I can to ease his life, but somehow the atonement never catches up to the sin."

"Have you also prayed to have a child?"

She looked at him strangely. She was calmer now, although there were still tears. "I have prayed many times in England."

"Then pray again, here. Your Anglican God has no authority on these shores. He stops at our twelve-mile limit. In America, different gods prevail."

"I do not know whether you are serious or not. If you are mocking me, you are not what I thought. But since you have been only kind, I will take it you mean what you say kindly. I will do as you say, but this is the only thing that will help me."

Madelyn reached out and gently squeezed his penis. With her forefinger she took the residue of semen from the tip. She held her finger to the gas lamp and looked intently at it, as if she were examining the sparkle of a diamond. "To think this little gives life," she said. Then she put the finger full length into her vagina.

The gesture alarmed Beckwith, but he said nothing. Madelyn was the first woman who had ever aroused him thus. He was willing to pay the consequences. He would not surrender her, not yet. However, he would be cautious.

Then Madelyn lowered the brightness of the lamp. "Hollis, you have made me very happy. But that was on one side; now do me on the other." And with that, she turned over and placed a pillow under her thighs. She spread-eagled, her face disappearing into the folds of the sheets, leaving him to look at a mass of disheveled brown hair. Beckwith shrugged. What else could he do, but oblige? She was, after all, an English lady.

12

JANUARY–MARCH 1847

FORDHAM VILLAGE
AND NEW YORK CITY
(Tenth Street and Batavia Street)

Virginia Poe was luxuriant in the linen gown. And her black hair was parted and smoothed meticulously to either side of her forehead. The delicate eyelids were closed and the pale face showed a whiter luminosity beneath the skin, as if to contradict to her viewers that she was really dead.

They all knew her time had come. Two days before she had had an attack of such severity that she almost suffocated in her own blood. Virginia's terrible suffering ended on the night of January 30, 1847. She was twenty-four, the same age at which Poe's mother and brother had died.

Mrs. Shew had gone back to the city. She hastily returned with the lustration garment, a linen gown from her own closet, after being summoned the next day. Later she washed and dressed the frail body. Then the coffin was nailed closed and placed on Poe's writing table, now centered in the small parlor between the two windows. Two shafts of gelid daylight touched either end of the coffin.

Coincidentally, a few days before, a familial contingent had arrived from Baltimore for a visit. There was Poe's sister, Rosalie, and two cousins, Eliza Herring and Mary Devereaux.

As the informal cortège left the cottage, an icy wind enveloped it. There were not many in the procession. They were led by a weeping Mrs. Clemm and a dazed Poe, followed by Rosalie Poe, Eliza Herring, Mrs. Shew, Nathanial Parker Willis (an editor-writer and the poet's best friend), Father Edward Doucet (a Jesuit priest from nearby St. John's College, who had befriended the writer), the Valentines (their kindly landlords), and Beckwith. Mary Devereaux stayed behind at the cottage to receive late visitors, but no one else came.

The casket was taken across a meadow and along a high road to a nearby Dutch Reformed church and placed at the lychgate. It was to be laid in the Valentine family vault at the rear of the church, for Poe, after paying his debts, had no money left to purchase a plot.

If Beckwith had known about the miserable preparations, he would have arranged for the funeral. To interfere now would be intrusive. So he made himself inconspicuous after being introduced to each of the mourners, offering his sympathy to Poe and Mrs. Clemm but speaking to no one.

The only thing which immediately concerned Beckwith was the date. He wanted Poe to be with him on the fourth of February, but it seemed that it was not meant to be. No doubt now that the poet would remain in Fordham past that day. No matter, he knew exactly where Poe was.

When the service was over, Beckwith left. As he walked back along the path over which the coffin had been borne, a morbid thought settled on him. Was it because Poe could not afford the plot that he did not bury his beloved child-bride? Or was it that in the fantastic realms of his anguish he imagined that Virginia, like Madeline Usher, would somehow force her coffin open, step from the crypt, and beckon her husband to accompany her to everlasting life? Or more calamitous for the poet. That Virginia's flesh would decay without her ever again being seen by Poe.

It was seven o'clock in the evening of the third day of February. The door of the narrow house at 51 Tenth Street opened in response to the knock.

"Mr. Beckwith. Please do come in." Mrs. Shew did not seem surprised to see him. Her lack of reaction might stem from her professional restraint as a nurse, Beckwith thought. As she placed his hat and greatcoat in the hall closet, he saw her profile. If he were ill, he could not hope for a more attractive attendant. She was a Poe ideal: petite figure, brunette coloring, symmetrical features, and vivacious blue eyes. Her hair was parted in the middle and bound simply with a red ribbon at the nape of her neck, and her dress was a gray barege, with a high neck, collar, and wide sleeves. Her figure went from a generous bust to a small waist and flowed out again. She smiled wryly. Her every move was one of assurance.

"Please, this way," Mrs. Shew said and led him into her father's consultation room. In it were a large desk and two chairs, one behind the desk and one to its right side; all the shelves were lined with medical texts. On the wall hung two diplomas.

"Since you have come to discuss Mr. Poe, and since my father is out on a call, I thought this a suitable room. Of course, if I am mistaken as to your purpose we can go to the parlor." She sat herself in the physician's chair behind the desk and looked directly into Beckwith's eyes. They were neutral, she determined. He does not faze easily, he needs a haircut, and he has a disconcerting effect.

It was not the reception Beckwith expected. His usual approach was to begin with the amenities, then the circuitous questions. Now he decided that shock would be the best technique to disrupt her composure.

"Are you and Poe lovers?"

It was the most indelicate question ever put to her, and despite herself she blushed. "Edgar does love me, but he also loves a half dozen other women who would give him the affection he so desperately craves. I admire him. He is a clever man, but when it comes to love, Edgar has as much subtlety as a McGuffey reader."

"Then why are you so attached to him?"

"I am attached to the family. I was asked to help, I have the ability, and I felt sorry for them. Besides, Edgar Poe has a great talent. Everything that can be done should be done for him. The Poes are such naïve people. They never should have come North; it is too uncongenial for them here. Do you know they call me their Loui? It started with Virginia, God rest her soul! He is Eddie, the mother was Muddie to both, and Edgar sometimes called his wife Sissie. Southerners have such a fondness for diminutive nicknames! Actually, I loathe Loui. I wince when they call me that, but they are so pathetic. If I were my usual gruff self, I would hurt them so. I am Marie Louise. I like Marie Louise. I prefer Marie. You may call me Marie."

She continued without pause.

"I have been repaid more than I dreamed. Edgar has written two poems in my honor and promises me a third. Of course, to be more accurate he has written one original poem and rewritten another. It is a favorite trick of his, you know. When he finds a passion—his latest is Mrs. Frances Sargent Osgood, the poetess —if he does not have the time to compose a new poem, he will revise an old one. There are already three Helens in his life. I wonder what the final count will be? Poor Edgar, he would be quite hurt to hear me talk so."

"Then you have treated him, Mrs. Shew . . . Marie? What is his specific illness?"

Unaware of her own gestures, she leaned forward in the chair, placing her right elbow on the desk and her hand to her chin, as one who dispenses advice in a professional manner. Beckwith attributed this mannerism to watching her father do the same thing over the years. Still, the dignity was her own.

"Firstly, Edgar has an affliction called romanticism, which makes the world a despairing place for him. Secondly, both his physical and mental composition make him prone to brain fever. Thirdly, I believe he has a lesion on one side of his brain. This is based on my having taken his pulse and consistently found that after every ten regular heartbeats there is a lengthy pause and then an intermittent pulse. It is also manifest in his twisted face, with its two different halves: noticeable, if one looks. My diagnosis was confirmed when my father's colleague, Dr. Valentine Mott of the School of Medicine of New York University, treated Edgar during his last illness. Fourthly, Edgar's fear that he might be going insane is substantial enough for Dr. Mott to refuse him drugs or tonics because these stimulants might accelerate this tendency. Even sedatives have to be administered to him with extreme caution.

"This is also supported by the vivid form of hallucinations Edgar has in his deliriums. He tells the most bizarre tales. How he wandered through Europe. That he wrote the *Wandering Jew* under the pseudonym of Eugène Sue in Paris and conversed with the literati of that city. How he fought a duel in Scotland and nearly perished; how Russian agents prevented him from enlisting in the Polish army. There were other fanciful tales. However, there is one strange note about these fits."

"And that is?"

"In the months I nursed him, Mr. Beckwith, he never varied his account. The details of his imaginary European sojourn remained constant."

"You have already answered my next question. Were there other dreams or incidents which he mentioned in his deliriums? But please, if I am permitted to address you by your Christian name, then you must call me Hollis. What is his present condition?"

"The death of his wife has made Edgar extremely despondent, and he shows symptoms of a recurrence of brain fever. He will undoubtedly be bedridden for a long time, probably several weeks."

"I am sorry to hear this."

"Hollis, do you not wonder why I have been answering your questions and volunteering information? You are thinking, Who is this querulous woman, this daughter of a doctor, whose ethics and background demand that she know better? No doubt you are disappointed that I am such an indiscreet person."

"Yes, ma'am . . . Marie. In truth I was wondering about it."

"You see, Hollis, I know who you are. Oh, I do not mean that you are the Police Superintendent and Edgar's present employer, but that you are his benefactor. When Dr. Reich went to Fordham in December, Mrs. Clemm assumed that I had sent him to examine Virginia. She expressed her gratitude to me. I made inquiries through Dr. Mott. I assure you Dr. Reich did not knowingly reveal a confidence. Any man who would do what you did has only the well-being of the Poes at heart. Tell me I am not wrong."

"Marie, the information you give me will be to Poe's benefit." Beckwith told the truth, but it was a weaseling truth. Her intent was kindness and she was guileless. He deceived her. It was necessary, but he still felt guilt. He decided it was time to leave. "You have been very helpful, Marie. And now I must go."

She rose and escorted him to the hall. "When will you call again?" Beckwith thought the question too emphatically worded, as if she demanded a commitment. It should have been, Will you call again?

"I do not know," he answered honestly.

"I see," she said evenly, "that you are having an illicit affair."

Jesus in Heaven, how did she know? He looked into her alert eyes. I go for months without meeting one appealing female; why is it my luck to meet two intelligent, alluring women at the same time? He said nothing.

"Logic is not the sole property of men," Marie said. "I know you are unmarried. That eliminates the wife. If you were courting another woman, you would have said, I am sorry but I am seeing Miss So-and-So. That eliminates a sweetheart. Forgive me if I am now immodest, but I am fair-looking. I believe you would have responded to at least one invitation from me. Yet you gave me no definite answer. Why? Because you are already occupied. Then why not mention it? You are a gentleman. It must involve some untoward situation, like a married woman. Therefore, your lover is another man's wife."

Beckwith again cursed his luck. He still said nothing, but stood before her somewhat humbly.

"I hope my candor does not repel you, Hollis. But if it does, that is all right too, for then you are not what I want. I suppose that is why I could so readily attend Edgar despite his objectionable qualities. In prose, he is an artist of the truth. He knows how to dissect subtle emotions, at least those of his male characters. A woman's body may be different, but her mind is essentially the same. There is an "Imp of the Perverse" in me. I must tell you the truth even if it is to my detriment, even if you think me less the woman. Will you hear me, Hollis?"

Do I really have a choice? It was a rhetorical question, Beckwith thought. But it was interesting, so let us continue.

"I have never had a lover, not even my husband. He was a coarse man whose taste was as vulgar as his sole object in life, making money. He was considerate in one thing: He died in the third year of our marriage. The irony of this match was that I chose him myself. My father disapproved. He thought Mr. Shew without refinement and warned me not to proceed. But I was strong-willed. So much for love and certainly the finish for marriage, I decided. And this distaste held me until recently.

"Lately I have been extremely unsettled. I have subjugated my bodily instincts too long. Yet am I unnatural because of my marriage trauma? I care nothing for a home and children. I was most happy to be immersed in other matters.

"Then I saw you at the funeral. I made inquiries, deviously guided conversations—all to the end of knowing more about you. What else shall I say, what else need I say?"

She did not wait for an answer, which was just as well, since Beckwith did not intend to speak.

"However, there is one thing I am obdurate about. Whatever else my feeling, I will not share any man. When you have finished your present affair, do call again. Meanwhile, as encouragement . . ."

She reached up and placed her arms around his back, for she had not the height to make his shoulders. She kissed him lightly, experimentally. She paused and touched her lips with her tongue like a connoisseur sampling a wine.

"It has been a long time since I have had a man's taste on my lips. It is more pleasant than I thought it would be. Once more, please."

This time Beckwith put his arms around Marie, lifted her off the ground, and pressed her against him so that he could feel the length of her. They kissed for many minutes.

"I do not know how it will end, Hollis, and for the moment I really don't care. But to end, it must begin. The next time you come we will start in the parlor."

———

Though not completely well, Poe had recovered sufficiently to dismiss the sensation of paramnesia. He assured himself that he had been in the office of the Police Superintendent before. He affirmed it by remembering the maps, the directories, and the flags in the sparse office on Chatham Street. Beckwith was not there, but then the appointment had been for five o'clock and the poet was twenty minutes early.

No, nothing much changed in the three months since he had first been there—except himself. He was more raddled.

Poe had mentally disintegrated on the night of his wife's funeral. There were fitful lamentations and then he cried. The next day he collapsed and was put into the bed in which Virginia had died. For two weeks he lay there, wildly ill with brain fever. Once he had to be restrained from darting out of the house in his nightclothes to search for his Virginia. When he was rational, he incessantly pleaded with Mrs. Clemm for morphine. Loui was there again to care for him, and Dr. Mott made a call.

Two weeks later, the writer was well enough to take walks.

154

He would make his way across the meadow through groves of cypress and willows into fields made winter-wet by the melting snow and cold rains of mid-February. He needed extra effort to reach the high ground along Kingsbridge Road where the Dutch Reformed church stood. There he would go thirty paces to the east of the rear porch to gaze, and sometimes prostrate himself, at Virginia's tomb. Occasionally, he would remember other graves: of his mother, Elizabeth Poe; of his first adult appreciator, Jane Stanard; of his foster mother, Frances Allan. All young women, made even younger now because he was older.

At other times, he ambled through the woods until he reached High Bridge, where he would look beyond the Harlem flatlands to the city. Twice he made his way to St. John's College, content to be in the presence of the stone buildings representing a religion more than a thousand years old. And it helped whenever he looked at his new talisman to inure himself against the unceasing hammerings—a ring of two gold circlets joined together, made from Virginia's and Muddie's wedding bands.

As if to coincide with his recovery, an aberrant southeast wind billowed in, bringing with it such mildness that it deceived the buds into appearing on the early flowering plants.

Poe wore his Spanish cape and sat in the raised islet of his cottage, bounded by scattered evergreens, scrawny lilac bushes, and a denuded cherry tree. Serpentine vines, some broken into parts, clung to the house like petrified brown snakes. He was not deluded by the illicit weather, for he knew that for him winters were meant to be long. In this mood, he began writing the elegy "Ulalume." Then the wanton current of balmy air righted its course and a rejuvenated winter destroyed the incipient spring. Once more the earth was dank and impenetrable. Once more he was back on Chatham Street.

"Poe, how are you?" Beckwith had come in. He held out his hand and noted the divided face. It was as Marie said; one had but to look closely.

In his highly nervous state, Poe could not bear to maintain

a conversation. He responded in fusillade fashion: Yes, it was time to continue the Garroter investigation; yes, he felt better; no, there was no need to apologize for summoning him, he was glad to get away from Fordham village; no, it really did not matter where (or even whether) he ate.

They went out of the Old Jail to Pearl Street and turned onto Oak. The conversation went on: Mrs. Clemm, Mrs. Shew, and where they might dine. It seemed to Poe that Beckwith had selected the restaurant, since they were proceeding in a particular direction.

Beckwith stopped in front of a house on the short block of Batavia Street, near the East River. He said he had business there, that it would not take long. Would Poe mind waiting for him? The door opened and a maid took their hats and coats. Beckwith went into a room on the right and Poe was led into the sitting room on the left.

Beckwith entered an empty room and quickly closed the door. The arrangement was that the house would be vacated for at least three hours, and after that the night's business would begin again. Of all the inquisitions to which Beckwith had exposed Poe, he regretted this the most. Still, it had to be done. He was already a month off schedule, and he really had nothing concrete to do except await replies to his correspondence. That there had been no garroting in February was, he felt, merely a reprieve. The fourth of March was three days off.

Beckwith had been to the Batavia Street house the week before, when he learned that the poet had recuperated. He would have dearly liked to close this place and all those like it in the city, but he knew he would undercut support for his Star Police. One step at a time. To make the force indispensable so that no amount of pressure would dissolve it was his objective; then on to the vices which corrupted the city.

He told the distinguished-looking Mrs. Hillsworth the type he wanted: American, young, dark coloring, small frame, pale complexion, refined looking, regular features, soft voice, and, if possible, intelligent. Five minutes later, the girl he had described appeared before him, with an added attribute, a serious mien.

"What is your name, girl?"

"Jewel, sir."

"Has Mrs. Hillsworth explained what it is you have to do?"

"Yes, sir. But I don't see that it differs from the others. I'm to take the gentleman upstairs, give him a drink, and entertain him."

"Not exactly, Jewel. You're to speak to the gentleman, give him a drink, and then take him upstairs. For if you do not let him imbibe, he may not go with you."

"I see, sir."

"Also, I will be in the closet, watching and listening."

"That's not unusual either. We have a lot of that around here. There's an extra charge for it."

"Yes, I know," said Beckwith. "I've already taken care of it. Here is something for you. There is no need to tell Mrs. Hillsworth about this."

"Thank you, sir."

"Jewel, there is some danger. It is possible that the man will become violent."

"There's that possibility with the others too," she replied, as she lifted her dress and tucked the money in her stocking.

"Don't be afraid. I will be there to protect you. The important things to remember are not to panic, not to speak any more than necessary, and not to give him more than two drinks. After the first one, he will be drunk, though he may not seem so. If he doesn't respond, give him another. Then lead him to your room and undress him. Wear a simple dress. Also, here are some poems. If you can't think of anything to say, just read. Now do you understand it all?"

"I don't understand it, sir, but I will do exactly as you say."

Being in the house again, it seemed like yesterday to Beckwith that he made these arrangements. He made his way to Jewel's room and ensconced himself in the closet.

157

There was a noise on the staircase, then a lurching sound just before the door opened. Poe came into the room, supported by Jewel. There was a cosmetic smile on his chalk face.

At first, Poe refused the wine, but the girl coaxed so charmingly it would be inhospitable not to join her. Then everything became gauzy; with the second draught, he experienced vertigo. It was worth it, for that exquisite creature was concerned for him.

> An opiate vapour, dewy, dim,
> Exhales from out her golden rim . . .

"Virginia, I fear I am unwieldy. Come help me with my clothes," Poe called. "Yes, upstairs, that is a good idea. My legs have strength, but I do not need them. I am celestial. Virginia, are you there? Yes, you are a jewel. That face, let me make you immortal; I have that power, you know. You shall be Helen.

> "First Helen, thy beauty is to me.
> Second Helen, thy beauty is to me.
> Third Helen, thy beauty is to me.

"Why not, why not? It is a perfect line. Is it not worth the repeating just as loving a woman bears repeating? Never mind, I have had enough of Helens. They are all wasted.

"I feel the closeness of your lips, Elmira. I stand in front of your unentered vault, Elmira; let me in. Virginia, I feel your lips on mine. I stand outside your vault, Virginia; let me in. Frances, I feel the ether breath of your mouth. Your vault is warm, Frances; let me in. Jane, I feel your tongue in my mouth. I did not want to come into your vault, but you forced me in, Jane."

Then the opalescence evaporated and the room became awash with tints and hues from gaseous globules and there was a superabundant silence.

"There you are. It is hard to see. But I can feel your little hand. Let me kiss it, Sissie. Oh, but your body, your body is a jewel. It has been so long, Virginia, so long. Now that you are healed, let me in. It is not wrong to love a cousin-sister-wife."

It was the day after Poe's spectacular seven-mile swim, and he walked in triumph at Mr. Burke's academy. Young Bob Stanard became his admirer. More important than gaining a friend whose family belonged to the leading social circle of Richmond, Bob took him home to meet his mother, Jane Stith Stanard.

She was his first Helen. Mrs. Stanard was not only beautiful but cultured. At twenty-nine, she looked uncannily like the miniature portrait of his mother. Also, although he loved Frances Allan, his foster mother, she could not compete with Jane Stanard in intellect. However, mother, foster mother, friend's mother, they were all from the same mold. Jane Stanard had regular features, dark coloring, a lofty forehead, sensitive lips, and a delicate manner. She often wore décolleté gowns revealing a pale throat and neckline. But it was the large lavender eyes, the searching empathetic eyes that drew him.

Edgar went often to her house. Mrs. Stanard would make him read his poetry. She was enchantingly prescient. He had only to intimate and she embraced the quintessence of his art. He was never to find the kinship with any other woman that he had with her. She was feminine perfection incarnate; she was also madness incarnadine.

All that we see or seem
Is but a dream within a dream.

The carriage was on the Petersburg road on an unseasonably warm March day. Mrs. Stanard was to get her son at the country home of a friend. Dismissing the Negro coachman, she invited Edgar to accompany her. They were about two miles out when she asked him to stop.

"Edgar, I did not realize how warm it was today. I am afraid I overdressed. There is a cool place here to pause awhile." She guided him down a trail through woods abounding with hyacinth to the edge of a small lake.

No footstep stirred: the hated world all slept,
Save only thee and me. (Oh heaven!—oh, God!)

"I came here often, Edgar, and I would wander through this, my domain. Sometimes I would run." Saying this, she discarded her parasol, took off her bonnet, and began to run. It was a game and he would play. She was surprisingly fast, but it was easy for him to keep pace. At last, out of breath, she threw herself down in a shadowed copse. And when she turned to him, the lavender eyes were ablaze.

Save only the divine light in thine eyes—
Save but the soul in thine uplifted eyes.

She lay in the grass, the sunlight peering between the overhang of the trees. "Come closer, Edgar. I have something to tell you," she said softly. "A secret I have told no other. Come lay your head on my chest so I can speak into your ear, for the others may be listening." To accommodate the gesture she slipped out of the top of her dress and pressed his head against her bare breasts. He recoiled but she held him savagely fast.

And I said: "She is warmer than Dian:
She rolls through an ether of sighs—
She revels in a region of sighs: . . ."

"I am a woman. Surely this is no secret," she whispered, her tongue flitting in his ear. "Yet men make it a secret. This is a woman's body; it feels the pain of a woman's body so it should feel its delights. I said to my husband, Do this and do that. And he was shocked. A lady was not meant for that, he adjudicated (he is a judge, you know). Do it, it was meant to be. You do it with the whores of Jonquil Street, I know it. They are women. It was meant to be. And he was exceedingly angry. It is an abomination, he said, you are highborn. Hypocrite, I replied. How can what is joy there be an abomination here? Lady and harlot, are we not both made from God's design? Or am I mad? He said,

I have my duty and you have yours and there is an end to it. Spewer of cant, you had your chance. You put it in and take it out. Now, keep it out.

"Sensitive soul, Edgar, sensitive mouth." And she pulled up her dress. The youth was horrified. There was not a single piece of underclothes. She put her tongue in his mouth. "Now make your talented tongue do more than say pretty words. Let me feel I have entered into the rightful paradise—otherwise let all the pretty words be condemned as lies." She placed her hands along his head and guided him down.

To think of—to do such a thing to any woman was beyond his comprehension. That one of her breeding should ask it was beyond imagining. Then he thought, Was she not a knowing woman? Is not part of love how love is done? How do I know? It must be, if she asks.

His tremulous tongue did its task between her legs. And his nostrils were full of the scent of hyacinth. He was too bewildered to know if he enjoyed it. Yet if it gave her pleasure, why not? She had given him much solace.

"Yes, I am proved. Why was I denied this? I will no longer be denied." It did not seem she was talking to him. Then she opened his trousers. "You are not ready, virgin. I will gird you, for it is a hard road to travel." And she took off his clothes and hers. She positioned him supinely and caressed him. Then she mounted him. "If they ask I can say I was not unfaithful. No man, other than my spouse, has entered me. But what they will not know is that I entered into another." And she laughed wildly.

"Come up, in despite of the Lion,
    To shine on us with her bright eyes—
Come up through the lair of the Lion,
    With love in her luminous eyes."

A month later Jane Stanard went insane. A year later she died in an asylum.

And the fever called "Living"
Is conquered at last.

But Edgar did not abandon Jane Stanard. Despite his fear of cemeteries, he forced himself to go, and there on her grave his tears fell.

"I am at your vault, Jane. I am ready, but it is too late."

Two years later he became informally engaged to Sarah Elmira Royster of Richmond. He decided to tell his soul mate of the mysteries (though not how he acquired them), how enormously happy he would make her on their marriage bed. In a fury, she slapped his face and told him that a lady would not be treated so. He apologized and in her young love she forgave him. When he became enamored of Mary Starr of Baltimore, he again repeated how he would delight her. She flushed, said nothing, and saw him no more. It was enough; how many times did he have to suffer? Jane Stanard was ablated from his memory—so much so that when Robert Stanard and his father, the Judge, called to congratulate him on his marriage to Virginia he had not a recollection of that adulterous, mad March day.

My love, she sleeps! Oh, may her sleep,
As it is lasting, so be deep!
Soft may the worms about her creep!

And he protested, "Why did you forsake me? What am I guilty of, Elizabeth Poe, Frances Allan, Jane Stanard? Let me in. I am lank and lonely. I wander among corpses."

By a route obscure and lonely,
Haunted by ill angels only . . .

"I remember now. Why did you deny me? Why did I let you deny me, Elmira Royster, Mary Starr, Virginia Clemm, Marie Louise Shew, Frances Osgood—Helen, Jewel, Madelyn. Let me in. What I would do to you all now. I have it within me. I would be let in."

> There the traveller meets, aghast
> Sheeted Memories of the Past—

And the bed in the upstairs room of the house on Batavia Street shook ferociously as if it were occupied by a poltergeist.

> Out of SPACE—out of TIME.

13

MARCH 1847

NEW YORK CITY
(The East Side and Chatham Street)
AND BORDENTOWN, NEW JERSEY

The cab traversed Sheriff Street for the third time since one o'clock. It transported its two passengers at irregular intervals through the rectangular area bounded by Rivington, Delancey, Chrystie, and Tompkins streets.

In reverse of their usual dispositions, it was Beckwith who was tense and taciturn and Poe who was pacific and inclined to conversation. The poet had felt tranquil ever since he awoke in the bedroom of Beckwith's home two days before. Why, he did not know. It was not as if something beneficial had happened to him in the interim. In fact, he could not remember anything after he had entered the house on Batavia Street and had raised the wine glass to his lips in the company of a pretty dark-haired girl. The writer did not regard this as strange, for in the past year he often had mental lapses which lasted for days. Usually when he regained his senses he was confronted by some embarrassing or humiliating incident. For this reason, he avoided inquiring what had actually taken place. When Beckwith did not mention it, Poe assumed that he had merely blacked out and been brought to Lafayette Place to recover.

And now on this day, the fourth of March, 1847, they were crisscrossing the area which was the scene of the first two Garroter murders, as hunters stalk a quarry that has backtracked on its trail.

The Police Superintendent had done all he could to minimize the risk of a third killing. He had doubled the number of men in these twenty-one blocks from the Bowery to the East River wharves and kept the previous night's watch on duty. He intended that all of them stay in the area of the two murders until midnight if necessary. Nor did he allow Poe out of his sight.

Beckwith had not expected anything to happen so early in the day, for the Garroter's pattern was to take his victim in the afternoon and dispose of her in the evening. But perhaps, if they were lucky, they would spot the Garroter. Actually, as far as Beckwith was concerned, there was no choice. There was nothing else to do but patrol and scrutinize.

Yet for all his precautions, Beckwith was full of foreboding. If he was wrong, there would be a terrible penalty.

The comments between the two men were sporadic, for Beckwith was looking hard and feared being distracted by inconsequential conversation. That he was restricted to the cab made the Police Superintendent testy. As the vehicle turned onto Rivington Street he suggested to Poe that they get out and walk for a time. Though still weak from his recent illness, Poe readily agreed.

It was a bright, crisp day. A rowdy wind ruffled the unwound awnings of the shops and nosily rampaged through the streets, upsetting loose articles and blowing them helter-skelter. So intent on his quest was Beckwith that he was assiduously gazing into every face and doorway.

Suddenly the poet exclaimed, "Beckwith, did you see him? It was Philip Lewissohn. He just went around the corner. What the devil is he doing here?"

"Are you sure, Poe?"

"I tell you it was he. I am going to check."

"Poe, wait for me. We will go together." But the poet began to run, easily outpacing Beckwith, and was far in front of his companion as he turned the corner onto Columbia Street.

"Poe, stop, wait for me," Beckwith called, oblivious of the stares of passersby. When this pleading failed to halt the writer, he shouted, "Come back, Poe. I order you to come back." It was useless. Beckwith then reached into his pocket and gripped the Haston. He thought about firing in the direction of the running figure but decided against it. It probably would not stop the monomaniacal Poe, and he would make himself even more conspicuous. All he could do now was to mutter futilely, "Poe, you damn fool, make sure you come back."

Beckwith was furious at himself, that he had allowed this to happen. He had worked it so carefully, staying close to the poet to prevent just such an occurrence. Returning to where the cab was waiting, he dispatched one of his men to pass the word that Poe was to be arrested on sight and taken to the Old Jail in manacles.

Beckwith sorely needed exercise but nevertheless reentered the cab in a symbolic gesture of self-confinement, as punishment for his negligence in permitting the poet to escape. For more than four hours he incarcerated himself in the vehicle, relentlessly searching, forcing himself to concentrate on the streets for a telltale sign. It was just after nightfall when a policeman found him and informed him that Sarah Lewissohn had been abducted.

After Beckwith sorted out the details in his office at the Old Jail late that night, he had ambivalent feelings. The message he received concerning the abduction was true, but the aftermath was puzzling.

As nearly as he could determine, this was what had happened: Sarah Lewissohn had been an afternoon visitor of Joan Jay. Sometime before five o'clock she left for her home on King Street, some eight blocks away. As the girl passed the Dutch Reformed church on Amos Street an arm reached out from an open gate in the high iron fence. It held her about the mouth so that she could not scream. As she was pulled onto the church grounds a cloth soaked in ether was put over her face. About an hour later, at six

166

o'clock, Sarah Lewissohn was discovered unconscious on White-hall Street. It seemed as if she had simply been dropped there by her abductor.

The only hint of the Garroter's real intent, Beckwith thought, was when he learned that earlier in the day the two young girls, admiring each other's dresses, had decided to exchange outfits. Also, he noted that Joan Jay and Sarah Lewissohn were of the same frame and coloring.

There was nothing more substantive in the information Beckwith gleaned from other sources. No one had been at the church, nor had the pedestrians on Whitehall Street at the time seen anything unusual.

Beckwith wondered why the Garroter—there was no reason to believe it was anyone else—did not strangle Sarah Lewissohn. Why did he abort this attempt? Was the madman's pattern changing? (That would be alarming.) Beckwith speculated that there was still a gesture involved: evidently, the Garroter had gone to the trouble to transport Sarah Lewissohn from Amos Street in the northwest district across the city to Whitehall Street.

His thoughts were interrupted by the sergeant of the watch, who opened the door and informed him that Poe had been arrested and was now in the building. Beckwith walked one floor up and entered through the solid metal door leading to the isolated wing to which he had ordered Poe taken.

When he saw the Police Superintendent in the narrow stone corridor, Poe tried to approach Beckwith but was restrained by the two policemen escorting him. "These louts have arrested me," the author said indignantly. "Tell your men who I am. Tell them I am working with you."

"Did you find Philip Lewissohn?" Beckwith replied, dismissing the entreaty.

"No. I looked everywhere. He just vanished. But don't you see? It proves my point. If he were innocent, he would have stayed and made himself known."

"Then Lewissohn was not in your company nor you in his.

As a matter of fact, Poe, you cannot even be sure it was he."

"I would swear it was Lewissohn, but I cannot verify it."

"Or even that you really saw anyone at all?"

"What do you mean?"

Beckwith ignored the question. "Why did you not return to me?"

"Because I felt then as I do now, like an idiot. After running off like that and then the fruitless search, I just wanted to go off and get drunk."

"But you did not."

"No. I knew I would only make myself more the fool. I decided instead to search for the Garroter on my own."

"Did you see anyone who knows you or who would vouch for your whereabouts during that time?"

"I cannot think at this moment. I wandered about. I don't remember exactly where I was or what I did. I cannot think now. All I have in my head is that if it gets out that I was brought to the Old Jail under these circumstances I will be utterly humiliated."

"Poe, you are a fool. You deliberately ignored my plea to stop. You will recall that when we entered into this arrangement I specified that you were to do exactly as I said. Now you will find out what it means not to heed me. Lock this man up."

"Beckwith, what are you saying?" The policemen now held Poe forcibly, for he had almost succeeded in breaking free.

"Edgar A. Poe, also known as Edgar Allan Poe, alias Henri le Rennet, alias Edgar A. Perry, who also uses the name Eugène Sue, I arrest you for the murders of Angelina Van Courtlandt and Alicia Schuyler, for the abduction of Sarah Lewissohn, for the murder of Mary Rogers, and for the theft of federal government property, your guard coat, which you stole from West Point."

"What? What?" came out of the astounded poet. "What the devil are you talking about?" All that Poe could initially think of with all the accusations charged to him was his name. "I used Edgar A. Perry to enlist in the army. Henri le Rennet is paronomasia, a word game. It means Henry the Reborn in French, which is how I felt when I left my foster father's house. And see how wrong you are; I have never used the name Eugène Sue."

"You did in your fits," responded Beckwith.

"Good God, even in my hallucinations I have no privacy!"

"Every part of a man's life becomes the public record when murder is concerned," Beckwith responded.

"Murder, murder," Poe raged. "You accuse me of murder. What nonsense is this? What do I have to do with the murders of Angelina Van Courtlandt and Alicia Schuyler?"

"You killed them, Poe. Your disposition is that of a murderer. You are sick, physically and mentally. You are obsessed with death. Most of your work reveals this. You have also written that there is no more appropriate subject for poetry than the death of a beautiful woman."

"But why would I want to kill these girls?"

"You are violently unstable. You have a history of uncontrollable fits of rage, particularly under the influence of alcohol. You frequently have lapses of memory. These periods of blacking out are getting progressively longer. Your motive could be your fury against a world which has treated you unjustly. Somehow these rich and pretty girls represent to you your lost opportunities, the unrequited promise of your youth. What does it matter? Madness generates its own motive."

"And Mary Rogers, who was murdered six years ago, how does she fit into this?" Poe asked sarcastically.

"I have looked into that case quite thoroughly. Your account was really an extraordinary piece of detection. It was too clever. I asked myself, How could he have deduced the solution? Then I learned that you knew Mary Rogers, that you frequented the tobacco shop on Nassau Street where she worked. You are a philanderer, Poe. Undoubtedly, you must have tried with her. She rejected you and you were furious. You wanted revenge. I also found out that you were at the Elysian Fields in Hoboken where her body was discovered. You went there ostensibly to investigate the murder, but probably to destroy any trace that would lead to you. Mary Rogers was strangled. She was your first victim. But you are the consummate egocentric. You had to show the world your brilliance by writing 'The Mystery of Marie Rogêt,' even if it meant implicating yourself."

"Excellent reasoning," Poe said contemptuously. "Except for one thing. It is not true."

"Of course, the Mary Rogers case is too old for me to attempt to prove what I say," Beckwith commented. "But if I were to suggest in public that you murdered her you would be persecuted by the mob, if not prosecuted by the State. However, you did know the others, the Garroter's victims and the abducted girl."

"But I was never near any of those girls when they died."

"And how can you prove that? You were in the city when Angelina Van Cortlandt was murdered."

"Yes, but I was ill in Fordham village when Alicia Schuyler was killed."

"And who would testify that you did not leave? Your wife, who is now dead? Mrs. Clemm? Your mother-in-law's word would be worthless in court. The prosecutor would merely have to point out her years of selfless devotion to you and suggest that she would gladly commit perjury to save you. She would not make much of a witness in your defense. It would not matter, in any case. I have kept from you sworn testimony from people who saw a man fitting your description at the scene of Alicia Schuyler's death. Also, another witness has identified you as the man hurrying away from the place where the body of Angelina Van Cortlandt was found."

"But, but," sputtered the disoriented Poe, hoping that he could trivialize the serious charges by concentrating on a petty one, "I took the guard coat only because I had an ear infection and it was the middle of winter. My foster father refused to send me money. I had no clothes. But I had nothing to do with these murders."

"You ran away yesterday on the flimsy excuse that you saw

Philip Lewissohn. It was really because you wanted to get away from me to commit your next crime at its fixed time."

Beckwith nodded to the two policemen; they opened the door to the cell and shoved Poe in.

"But it isn't true," cried Poe, his defiance gone. "You cannot prove any of it." Even as he uttered these words, the despair in them was nullified, for sound was anechoic in this part of the Old Jail.

"The public is eager for the capture of the Garroter. With your reputation, Poe, I need prove nothing, only intimate. You would be convicted," said Beckwith. He turned and walked slowly down the corridor.

"But I am innocent!" Poe shrieked at the diminishing figure of the Police Superintendent.

"I know," replied Beckwith, closing the iron door behind him.

The bars of his cell became spastic and the space between them opaque. Dark red and purple spots came hurling straight at Poe just before he fainted.

———

That night Beckwith slept with Madelyn. But an hour before dawn he was already dressed and gone from Lafayette Place. He crossed to Perth Amboy by ferry and from there took the railroad to the Delaware River, then boarded the ferry to Philadelphia, a trip which lasted the day.

The next morning, Beckwith hired a horse and rode northeast on the Old High Road parallel to the Delaware River on the Pennsylvania side. Past Bristol, at Kirbridges Ferry, he crossed into New Jersey. It had not rained in the area for many days, and he had a dry, dusty journey.

Now, two miles outside of Bordentown, he was standing on the high level ground of the estate known as Point Breeze. It was to this place overlooking the gently winding Delaware that his agent had traced Count Motier.

Beckwith was awaiting the reaction to the announcement of

his arrival. From the entrance to the sumptuous château, with its unusual belvedere, Beckwith could see another lavish three-story building, which he had been told was a guesthouse, the Maison du Lac. Surrounding the villa was an ornate park. To one side was a labyrinth of manicured hedges, and for a thousand yards out stood disciplined rows of shrubs and trees. Interspersed in this grandly designed landscape were marble statuary and four ponds inhabited by waterfowl. This symmetry, this opulence, produced in Beckwith an intense sense of artificiality. The total effect, he decided, reminding himself he was in New Jersey, was ludicrous.

Despite a disdain for his immediate surroundings, Beckwith wished he could groom himself before being presented. It was a matter of personal pride.

A servant returned, begged Beckwith to enter, and took his riding coat. Yes, he was informed, he would be received. There could be no other response, Beckwith thought. A European political exile in America would never feel so secure as to refuse to see a police official. Thus it was that three minutes later Beckwith entered a large drawing room and was politely greeted by the master of Point Breeze, Joseph Bonaparte, Napoleon's older brother, the man who had been King of Spain.

14

MARCH–JULY 1847

NEW YORK CITY
(Chatham Street, Hanover Square, and Forty-second Street)

It was his fourth afternoon in the Old Jail, and Poe was resting his head against the soft pillow on his cot. If this is what it is to be in prison, he thought, I should like to spend more time here. He was as comfortable as a guest at the fashionable St. James Hotel on Fifth Avenue. Although he had been held incommunicado for the entire period, all newspapers were made available to him. The jailer brought him the best of meals from the local restaurants, and he was daily queried if he desired any special dish. Also, for each of the previous three days, Dr. Reich had appeared to examine him. When Poe asked the physician to convey a message to Muddie, the doctor gave him an ambiguous response.

Although unhappy about being in jail, the poet sardonically observed that he had finally arrived at the state he had yearned for—all his wants were being satisfied. He had just about everything, in fact, except his freedom.

Still, even in this ironic musing, Poe was not deceived. He had finally learned. He knew now that Beckwith was responsible for all this, was his nemesis. Who else could constantly devise situations of such diabolical contradictions to torment him? Beckwith's singular evil was to inflict pain through kindness. There pulsed through the poet an enmity for the man.

Poe heard a sound in front of his cell. It was time for Dr. Reich's visit. Looking up, however, he began to shake. Could it be that merely by thinking about him he had conjured up his tormentor? There stood Beckwith. The writer bolted into the upright position.

"Good afternoon, Poe. I trust you have been treated well?"

The poet did not reply. He stared at his persecutor. He was angry but calm, and determined that no longer would his emotions be ruffled.

"Demon, what new tortures have you devised for me?"

"Come now, Poe, do not be angry. I will explain all."

"Go away, you can no longer deceive or hector me."

"There is no need for either any more, if you will come with me."

"I will go nowhere with you. I am safer with these bars about me than in your protection."

"You inadvertently speak the truth, Poe. I *did* provide the bars for your protection, as I have the comforts for your stay, and I can understand your anger. However, if you will allow me to explain—"

"I will allow nothing but your leave."

"Poe, remember I have it in my power to ruin you. Do not force me to use intimidation. If after my explanation you are not only satisfied but grateful for what I have done, you are free to go. This I promise."

"If you can make me display gratitude after all I have suffered because of you, then you really are a demon. With this understanding, I will allow myself to be released."

Beckwith's reaction to Poe's hauteur was silent amusement. After they arrived at the Police Superintendent's office, the writer displayed his hostility by sitting rigidly and refusing to look at his persecutor. In his restless fashion, Beckwith moved from one end of the room to the other while he spoke.

"Poe, nothing I previously recounted was untrue, although

I exaggerated certain parts. Why this is so you shall presently learn.

"At the time Angelina Van Cortlandt was murdered, several witnesses observed a man with your likeness, completely in black and wearing a Spanish cape, in the vicinity of Rivington Street. At the time Alicia Schuyler was murdered, an identical description was obtained from several pedestrians. It was dark and the man moved quickly so they could not make out features. Nevertheless, the witnesses agree that he was of medium height, perhaps five feet, five inches, and thin. He was garbed in black and wearing a Spanish cape. In both instances your distinctive silhouette was describ—"

"But I told you—" interrupted the poet.

"Poe, please. Hear me out. Then you are welcome to say what you like. Additionally, the laborer, James Lewis, identifies you from a daguerreotype as the man leaving the place where he found the body of Alicia Schuyler on Delancey Street.

"One identification is circumstantial, two identifications defy coincidence. In other words, you were placed at the scene of both Garroter murders. Ordinarily, you would have been brought in for questioning immediately. I have no doubt that you would have been placed under arrest on suspicion of homicide. After all, it was not difficult to connect the description of the Garroter with you. You are a public figure, and—how shall I say it, Poe?—you have made yourself prominent in other ways. But these were not ordinary murders, nor were the victims or the mode of the crime ordinary. This matter became far too important for usual procedures.

"If you were guilty, to bring you in after the Van Cortlandt murder would have alerted you that you were under suspicion. If you were innocent, then certainly, for your own protection, I would need proof of that too. If you decided to run, that was no problem. You are a very traceable person. Meanwhile, should there be another murder I intended to prepare myself."

175

"Rather callous on your part, Beckwith, that you would be willing to expend another life," the poet interrupted, disregarding the fact that the Police Superintendent had safeguarded his rights and reputation.

"I was uncertain whether it would come to that, but I suppose it could be viewed in that manner," Beckwith responded. "Admittedly, it would be embarrassing to have another murder committed while the man I arrested was in jail. You are quite correct, Poe; it was better to be circumspect than have my career terminated.

"Meanwhile, I was having you investigated and formulating a plan predicated on the assumption that you were the Garroter. However, after studying your dossier there were several points which struck me as odd. And being with you these past four months has confirmed my inclinations.

"In you, more so than in most people, there is a pronounced dichotomy of the rational and the irrational. When rational, you are a clever, even cunning, man. If you were the killer, why did you not attempt to disguise yourself? Surely you knew that after 'The Raven' was published you would be recognized from your illustrated portrait and the particular garb you affect. Therefore, I deduced that if you had committed this murder it was not as a conscious act.

"Let us then consider the irrational possibility: The Garroter must be insane. Yet it is a special kind of madness, not obvious to those around him. What is the nature of your fits or illnesses? Brain fever, which incapacitates you; alcohol, which causes you to act in an uncontrollable manner. Both types of debilitation occur irregularly, without pattern. Hardly the hallmarks of the meticulous Garroter.

"Also, the Garroter undoubtedly has the appearance of a normal man but is sexually perverse. Your reputation is that of a necrophile, but your sexual inclination is that of a normal man."

"How do you know this?" blurted out the startled Poe.

"Let us just say I have examined every possible aspect of your

176

connection with this case," replied Beckwith. "Also, could you have had the opportunity to do the killings? In the Van Courtlandt killing, the answer would be yes; in the Schuyler murder, the answer would be no. You could not possibly have known about the Literary Liaison gathering that day since you were ill at Fordham village and the invitation was still in the West Farms post office. I checked and it was. Then there was the matter of the Five Points—"

"Yes," Poe interrupted again. "I wondered about that useless and dangerous venture."

"It was a favorable trip for you, Poe, for it helped affirm your innocence. First, you could not take a life under even the most justifiable circumstances. That is hardly the disposition of a murderer. Second, I spoke the truth that night. My informer could not leave the Five Points without danger. Thus we went to him. You were taken along to be identified. As you recall, the note I was given read, *The Garroter is not here. I have not seen him before.* The first sentence verified that the Garroter was not of that area; the second sentence absolved you of any connection with the murders as far as the Five Points underworld was concerned. This being so, what remains? A man who looks like you, but is not you. What is the conclusion? That whoever the Garroter is, he is deliberately making himself resemble you."

"Your premise is based on intuition," Poe observed, even though he was not helping his own cause. "With a witness giving positive identification, how can you be so certain it was not me?"

"Ah, Poe, when one uses deduction, nothing is certain. Logic is untidy when applied to life. Reason is only infallible in fiction. Only with your inimitable Dupin is there assurance that all the bewildering strands will come into place. I use deduction but do not depend on it. I must rely on facts, and for that an organization is essential. Nevertheless, deduction as a starting point has its place. Which brings us to your guard coat."

"The guard coat," said the poet in disgust. "Am I to be harangued on that count again?"

"Be at ease, Poe," Beckwith responded, almost laughing. "The statute of limitations has long expired on that act. I merely brought it up the other day to harass you. My purpose was the same when I charged you with the murder of Mary Rogers. Though you must admit that in the circumstances it appears more than coincidental that you knew her. However, taking the guard coat was probably one of the luckier acts of your life. Let us assume that the Garroter is attempting to blame you for his murders. For my part, even though he did an excellent job of duplicating your appearance, he failed. Why? Because while your other apparel is still in fashion and readily available from any tailor shop, the guard coat is of unique cut and material. Since it was taken from West Point more than sixteen years ago, there is none like it. You have only two outer garments, your Spanish cape and your guard coat. You wear nothing else. The Garroter probably would have worn a guard coat, but there is no way of obtaining one. Therefore, when all the witnesses recalled that the suspect wore a Spanish cape in the middle of winter I knew that you were not that man."

"If that was your conclusion, why was it necessary to treat me so unjustly?" Poe asked, unctuous with innocence.

"Because deduction, no matter how valid, is not evidence," Beckwith replied. "It was essential that I be with you during the fourth day of the month. Had you remained with me, it would have been irrefutable that you were not the Garroter. However, you chose to disregard me. Thus, while you are not guilty in my estimation, neither are you incontestably innocent, should all the facts of this case be revealed. You were jailed to impress upon you that I am to be heeded. This is my last warning, Poe. Do not cross me again or the consequences will be harsher."

"I have been thinking about the attempt on Sarah Lewissohn's life," the poet said, knowing that he would comply the next time but too proud to acknowledge it. "The Garroter could have killed her, but apparently she had some quality that did not conform to the rigid specification his victims must meet."

"Precisely, Poe. This is the reason I believe he returns to the same girls, even though the danger to himself grows with each attempt. Which brings us to another suspect."

"Count Motier, whose real identity you have determined. However, you are uncertain as to whether he is the Garroter."

"I see that jail has not diminished your deductive skills. How did you know?"

"There are only two suspects in this case who travel. Townshend's duties take him in all directions. Your investigators could make inquiries about him. Thus he would not qualify for your personal attention. However, as I recall from his dossier, Motier appears to go to only one destination. What would be so urgent as to take you out of the city except the Garroter? I was in Motier's quarters and saw his preparations for travel and also spied your man watching him. Evidently you discovered his destination and decided to investigate yourself. You have come here directly from the station, for some fine railroad soot remains on your jacket. I suspect that whatever it is you learned, it was not determinative. If it had been, you would have arrested Motier and would not be wasting time speculating with me."

"I was at Point Breeze, Poe."

"The capping of an architectural fantasy. It is magnificent. An anachronism in this country."

"More an anomaly," Beckwith riposted. "So you have been there?"

"Yes, in the autumn of 1840, when I was living in Philadelphia. The Count de Survilliers, as Joseph Bonaparte then titled himself, invited me. A cultured man and a munificent host. He is lavish with everything, as you undoubtedly found out."

"You, too, could also afford to be generous if you had absconded with the treasury of Spain, looted the art of Europe, and implanted a fortune in gems in the forests of Switzerland."

"Your political prejudices are causing you to malign this misunderstood and kindly man," replied Poe, with a sly smile, for he wanted to twit his infuriatingly self-confident colleague.

"Quite the contrary," Beckwith said coolly. "Those of us who advocate a republican form of government should be grateful to the Bonapartes. Particularly Napoleon, who was the consummate democrat."

"Why this paradoxical assessment?" asked Poe blandly.

"Because Napoleon demonstrated that a man need not be an aristocrat or wealthy to become a monarch. Is that not inspirational to a commoner in Europe? Even in America the most a man can hope to be is President."

Poe looked at him and laughed.

"For all I've said about old King Joseph, he did have a certain graciousness," Beckwith conceded. "And he was cooperative. So it was relatively easy to find that our Count Motier is actually Pierre Mailliard, the son of Louis Mailliard, Joseph's private secretary. Louis has been in Europe these past two years, involved in certain negotiations. It seems that the boy grew up in the Bonaparte household and acquired such gentlemanly accomplishments as dueling and overspending. Joseph Bonaparte knows the young man is a wastrel, but indulges him because of his father's long service. So we now know Motier's source of revenue. However, Joseph was unaware that the young man was masquerading as Lafayette's nephew. He was further distraught when I informed him of Motier's current escapades."

"Mailliard probably took the Motier identity," the writer observed, "because a connection with Lafayette would be prestigious to the family of an heiress."

"Joseph said he would refuse further assistance to this pretender. Imagine, Poe, the word 'pretender' coming from the mouth of a Bonaparte. But I dissuaded him. It is to my advantage that Mailliard not be found out."

"A good decision. You would not wish to alarm the Garroter. The best chance to capture him is if nothing changes. Also, if I know you, Beckwith, you are going to have Joseph Bonaparte's story verified through your French sources."

"That is so."

"I understand that you direct a secret communications apparatus which allows you to learn events before they become common knowledge. How do you do it?"

"Your statement is hyperbole. Keeping current is a necessity in politics and in criminal matters. You too could have foreign connections easily. I will prove it to you. In the prospectus for your magazine, the *Stylus*, you announce correspondents in London, Paris, and Vienna. If you had the capital to inaugurate your publication, would you actually use such correspondents?"

"Certainly, there are always people eager to do this work," the poet replied.

"You see. Only I retain them to collect information instead of for literary matters. I also select the fastest route by which this material is to be forwarded to me. In this manner, I have news two or three days before it is generally known."

"No doubt you are checking into the background of our other acquaintances, and I suppose they are being watched."

"That is correct, Poe."

"Have you then eliminated Motier as a suspect?"

"Why should I?"

"What profit would there be for a fortune hunter to kill prospective brides?"

"We are not seeking a rational person," Beckwith replied.

"Nevertheless, I contend that our list of suspects has narrowed," countered Poe. "There are only three remaining: Moran, a sexual pervert; Philip Lewissohn, whom I placed in the neighborhood of the crime; and Richard Townshend, who seems least likely to be the Garroter. If this were a story, it is he who would be guilty. I discount his wife. I know you disagree. I presume Madelyn Townshend is being watched?"

"Well, Poe, put it this way. She is being closely surveyed."

The author thought he detected a nuance of levity, even conceit, in the Police Superintendent's tone. What was the connection between the two?

"We must wait for the dispatches from Europe," Beckwith

said. "But we must also continue the search in the city and be especially wary on the fourth day of each month. Now that you know your hazardous situation, I hope you will trust me. By the way, did you ever suspect that this investigation was directed against yourself?"

"I would be the last to suspect, when I know myself to be innocent," Poe said.

Beckwith stopped his pacing. "Are you hungry? We could have dinner now."

"I appreciate your offer," the poet replied. "My only hesitation is that the last time we were supposed to have dined together, I don't remember having eaten."

They moved to the door. Poe hesitated. He did not want to discuss the subject but was overcome with curiosity. "One thing more, Beckwith. When the world thinks I am a necrophile and as I have cultivated that reputation, how do you know that I am sexually normal?"

———

Beckwith knew the identity of the Garroter. Or at least it was evident to him from the dispatch he had received late the night before. Nonetheless, a heavy uneasiness pressed him. The case had been drawn out for three more months because of the distance between New York and the European capitals.

The situation was further unsettling. The investigation overseas had uncovered something more diabolical than murder. The Garroter now represented an evil of such magnitude that it crossed national boundaries and involved the highest levels of a foreign government.

The noises of the Fourth of July celebration were distracting. A speaker's platform had been erected on Chatham Street for the occasion. Beckwith did not know which was more stifling, the oratory or the heat, but it was too hot to close the window. From the Battery, fireworks burst in the darkling sky.

At least nothing would happen this day, Beckwith thought. It was past time for the Garroter to act. At that moment, the door opened and the sergeant of the watch hurried in.

"Sir, we just heard. Officer Reardon has been stabbed to death and Miss Livingston has disappeared."

So this *was* to be the night. Of course. The Garroter had needed time to familiarize himself with the policemen guarding Joan Jay and Priscilla Livingston. Once he eliminated the protection, it would not take much to ensnare his unsuspecting victim.

Beckwith ordered the sergeant to bring the prisoner to him. Soon afterward, the officer returned with his charge, clad in unseasonable black.

"Ah, Poe, it is beginning to seem natural to have you in my jail," the Police Superintendent commented.

"I hope you will not think me ungracious if I say that I do not find that remark humorous," the writer responded.

"You are now cleared of the Garroter murders. The jailer and the sergeant will testify to your having been locked in the upstairs cell since midnight."

"Then the Garroter has taken another victim."

"Precisely, Poe. We must find him before he kills Priscilla Livingston." Beckwith sat on his desk and stared intently at the map of the city, in which three red pins had been stuck.

"I believe I know how the Garroter transports his victims without detection," the writer remarked.

More fireworks exploded. Slivers of color heaved upward, then became ashes drifting in the heavy summer night. Beckwith silently cursed the raucous oratory in the street, which was disrupting his thoughts.

"There is only one way," Poe continued. "By cab, which would seem natural in any part of the city, day or night. Since it is enclosed, it becomes a compartment to commit his foulness."

"Have you verified it?" asked Beckwith.

"I checked every stable in the city. The Garroter went to a different place for each occasion, but the order was the same. The cab was engaged the week before for the fourth day of the month and returned by eleven o'clock. The dates match the days of the two murders and the abduction. I have also obtained descriptions of the hirer, and they are identical."

"You knew this before, Poe. Why did you not tell me?"

"Because, from the description, I could have been the man who hired the cabs."

"So you were not going to further incriminate yourself. You offer me this information now that you are exonerated."

A torrent of patriotic haranguing came from the speaker below. Suddenly Beckwith stopped, stared at the poet, and rose to his feet.

"That phrase. Did you hear it? These *thirteen colonies*. Of course, that is the answer. Look at the map where the three red pins mark the locations of the Garroter crimes: *Rivington, Delancey,* and *Whitehall* streets."

"You have the advantage, Beckwith; the streets have no significance for me."

"That's because yours was a classical education and you don't know American history, Poe. This case is more than sexual perversion. The girls were killed in sacrificial vengeance, as symbolic immolations. Or so this madman reasons."

Beckwith's fingers touched the name of every city street on the map. "Come, Poe, there is not a moment to waste. I know where the Garroter will be."

"How can you be sure?"

"Because there is only one place left he can possibly go," Beckwith replied, reaching for his pistol in the desk drawer. "Hanover Square."

They stood in the shadow of the mall in the center of Hanover Square. From there, they could view the streets leading into it. (Their cab and driver were on Front Street, out of sight.) Beckwith had reasoned that the Garroter would approach from the east to avoid the holiday throng between the Battery and City Hall Park.

The two men had hurried from the Old Jail and pushed their way through milling crowds on Chatham Street so thick it was impossible for traffic to pass. They reached Spruce Street before

184

they were able to engage a cab. Now they waited in the deserted square, which was dominated by commercial buildings and banks.

There were continuous explosions in the sky, for they were barely a half mile from Castle Garden, where the pyrotechnics were being hurled into the moonless sky. Poe was rigid, listening. Beckwith thought he looked terribly pale.

They heard the sound of hooves before they saw the vehicle. It stopped on Water Street, a short distance away. Minutes passed. A figure descended and was about to open the cab door when Beckwith dashed forward.

"Now, Poe, rush him," he called. "If he comes into the square, it will be with a body. If the girl is still alive, this is our chance to save her."

The silhouetted figure slammed the cab door shut when he saw the two men running toward him. Nimbly, he climbed into the driver's seat and turned the vehicle about. Beckwith fired a signal shot into the air, and their cab appeared. The two men got up beside the driver.

They sped along Water Street, onto John Street, and were pitched to the left. One wheel never touched the cobblestones, so sharp was the turn. They crashed through a construction barrier and were almost flung from their seats. When they turned from Pearl Street into Chatham Square, the thoroughfare was filled with people; as they approached the Bowery, the pedestrians increased. They were closing the gap. Then their cab slowed.

"What are you doing, driver?" Beckwith demanded.

"There are people here, sir. I can't go fast. I'll tip over, and then where will I be?"

"On the street, where you're going now," said Beckwith, and he pushed the man off the cab. "See me at my office tomorrow," he called, taking the reins. "Damn, Poe, he has gained on us." They were approaching Union Place when the poet felt their speed slacken.

"Why are we slowing?" he asked.

"Because we do not have a thoroughbred hitched to this cab.

185

If we continue at this pace, the horse will soon expire. It is enough to keep the Garroter's cab in sight. When his horse is exhausted, we will have him. Damn, he is doing the same."

The cab ahead was on the other side of Union Place when it stopped.

"What's that madman up to now?" Beckwith muttered.

"He's taking something out of the cab," Poe exclaimed. "My God, it's a body. He's put a body on the street. It is she, Beckwith. Stop. We must help her."

The Police Superintendent came to a halt near the prone figure on the pavement. The writer was about to jump down when the cab started up again.

"Beckwith, what are you doing? We must help that poor girl!" cried the bewildered poet.

"If she is dead, there is nothing we can do for her. If she is alive, others will come to her aid. Look back, you will see people hurrying to her. Poe, I know who the Garroter is. I could have taken him any time today. I maneuvered him into this position and, by God, I'm not giving him up now. One life is nothing compared to what is at stake. We are dealing not just with a murderer of women but with the would-be murderer of a nation."

He is coldhearted, the poet thought. I would not be his enemy.

The pursuit took them along the Bloomingdale Road onto Fifth Avenue. The streets were dark, for there were no gas lamps and few houses in this suburb. At Forty-first Street, the Garroter's cab swerved and turned on its side. A dark figure jumped from the top and rolled along the ground.

"His horse is dead. The Garroter is mine now," Beckwith said.

"There he is!" cried Poe, pointing to the base of the Croton Reservoir. They raced after the dark figure, who now had reached the Latting Tower and was climbing up the side of the skeletal structure.

186

Suddenly, Beckwith groaned and fell to the ground in pain. "Oh, God, why now?" he moaned. The poet bent over him. There was no indication of what had felled his companion.

"I have a cramp in my leg." Beckwith grimaced. "I cannot stand. The Garroter must not be allowed to escape. Here is my Haston. Shoot him. He must die."

Poe was perspiring. Simultaneously, the chill of his worst fevers came over him. When the proffered pistol came into his hand, he felt ill.

"I will not do it," he declared. "I have never killed anyone. And I will not now. You cannot make me commit homicide to suit your whim of vengeance."

"Poe, I beg you to believe me. This is not a matter of vengeance. There is no time to explain. He must die. Do what I say or you will regret it. I will destroy you."

The poet looked at him scornfully. "What calamity can you cause for me that I have not suffered already? I have one inviolate principle left, my belief in the sanctity of life. You shall not take that from me."

"You miserable pipsqueak, you pretentious fop," Beckwith articulated icily. "What have you ever done to prove yourself a man? You failed all who depended on you. You killed them with your egotism, with your addiction to alcohol and drugs. How could I have ever thought I could rely on you? You whom I credited to be a man."

The tirade stunned Poe. He could not believe these indecencies were being directed at him. "If I had the capability to kill, I would kill you now, Beckwith. But you will not provoke me. I will not become your assassin."

There was a pause, and Beckwith shouted as if he expected all New York City to hear him.

"What could I expect from an effeminate scribbler, who can only have an orgasm with words? You counterfeit masculinity. I know now what they say about you is true. That you never did consummate your marriage. Your wife went a virgin to her grave.

Yes, that is what they say. I believe them, Poe. For you are probably as impotent in bed as you are in action."

The poet was enraged. The false charges scalded him. In fury, he aimed the weapon at Beckwith. A bead of sweat fell into his eyes, and its saltiness made him blink. In that minuscule pause Poe recalled the man's kindnesses and his generosity, how expedient it would have been for the Police Superintendent to charge him for the Garroter crimes. Beckwith was wanting in many ways, but he was considerate. He was calculating, but he was just. He did not tell the complete truth, but he had never lied. Good God, the writer realized, this baiting is a ploy. If Beckwith is so desperate as to resort to taunting me, then killing the Garroter is as urgent as he says. Very well. But let him think he manipulated me once more. That will be my triumph.

Poe moved forward a few yards to make sure he was in range and then sighted in on the figure, who had now reached the third level. In the distance, the tail of a rocket streaked heavenward. In the brilliance of the burst, he fired.

The black figure climbed a few feet more and fell backward from the tower, striking one of the flagpoles. The wooden pole broke from its mooring, and man and flag became entwined in the drop.

"Good shot," Beckwith said, limping toward the black figure, which had come to rest face down. He examined the body for a pulse. Then the Police Superintendent took the Haston from the poet, reloaded, and fired twice at the tower. The two shots severed a flagpole, and it came plummeting down. "The British flag should be his shroud. He defiles the one he lies on." Beckwith rolled the body off the American flag, which was smeared with blood, onto the Union Jack. "Now let us go."

"Hold," said the author. "You know who he is, but I am unsure." Poe turned the corpse over and gasped. He was looking into his own face. He had murdered himself.

15

JULY 1847

NEW YORK CITY
(Greenwich Street)

They were waiting in the hallway of the house on Greenwich Street.

"How could I not know he was the Garroter?" Poe chastised himself.

"Do not underrate yourself," Beckwith consoled. "I would not have known either if I hadn't had the resources. Certainly, deduction can point the way and, in some cases, even bring a solution. However, as you wrote in 'The Murders in the Rue Morgue,' one needs a balance of elements for insight. To that proposition I would add, One also needs the proper resources."

"What makes you think we will find anything incriminating here?"

"Well, to use your own deductive technique, I would say it was in the nature of the man to record everything he did. There was a compulsion within him. He did everything with precision. Everything had an order. Such a personality must justify what it does. Also, he probably believed he would never be caught. Otherwise, why did he play with us by leaving hints, such as the gloves and the thirteen?"

"Which was also why he protected you from Motier," contributed Poe. "Such a personality would also relish the sport.

What is a game without an opponent? He did not want anything to happen to the one man who could challenge him."

"Townshend would have done the same for you." Beckwith laughed. "Of course, we speculate. But it is really unnecessary. My source informs me that there is correspondence related to this case. I was told this on the condition that the correspondence, if found, is to be delivered to my English connection."

"Who is?" asked Poe.

"Sir Robert Peel," Beckwith replied.

Madelyn Townshend came down the stairs. "I am sorry I kept you waiting, but I had already retired. Hollis, why are you here? What has happened? Mr. Poe, forgive me. I did not see you."

"Madelyn, I am sorry. Your husband is dead. I will tell you all in a few minutes. First, I must ask some questions."

What have we here? the poet thought. *Hollis? Madelyn?* It cannot be. It is outlandish. He has no emotions. How could any woman love him?

"Madelyn, did your husband have sexual relations with you?"

She flushed and stared unrespondingly at Poe.

"Madelyn, believe me, I would not embarrass you. It is essential that you answer truthfully. Never mind Poe. He is in my confidence. Whatever is said here will never be repeated. I promise."

"Richard never touched me from the day of our marriage."

"That confirms it. Madelyn, your husband was impotent, some extreme sort of sexual deficiency."

"So that is it," she said. "I thought it was disgust because I could not bear a child for him, after he was forced into this marriage by royal pressure."

"No. Your situation suited him perfectly," Beckwith theorized. "As long as you thought that, he had no reason to prove he was a normal man. Your husband was not in the city the day of the first Garroter murder. Or so you thought. On the afternoon

190

of Alicia Schulyer's murder you were never together, were you?"

"I was out in my male attire," she said. "If Richard knew of my nocturnal wanderings, he would have stopped me. So when he suggested that we say we were together that evening, I readily agreed. It saved me an explanation."

"In providing you with corroboration, he was providing for himself as well. Madelyn, where did your husband keep his papers?"

"In the upstairs study, I think. I cannot be sure. Richard requested that I not enter the room. I never did."

"Wait here, Madelyn," Beckwith said and hurried upstairs, followed by Poe. At the top of the landing he went to the right, opened a door, and closed it.

At least, Poe thought, Beckwith had the decency not to make love to her in this house. The Police Superintendent went to his left, tried another door, and went in, the poet behind him.

"What are we looking for?" the author asked.

"Papers, correspondence, documents, possibly in cipher and particularly with the word *Troy* as a heading. I'll take the desk; you look around the room."

Poe began his search in the obvious places. Nothing. He had started for the bookshelves when Beckwith, who had been rummaging through the bottom desk drawer, held up a thick dossier. "I have it. How neatly the papers are arranged in categories: correspondence, vouchers for disbursements and a listing of the recipients, personal notations. . . ."

The Police Superintendent read the first sheet: *I have no compunction in putting my thoughts on paper. I am a man without being a man. I am abhorrent and know it. I cannot help myself or what I do. But God will forgive me, for it is God who made me this way.*

As he finished each sheet, Beckwith put it face down on the desk. The writer waited impatiently. Minutes went by. Only once did Beckwith display a reaction. "The Queen, the bloody Queen," Poe heard him mutter.

"The plan is as ingenious as it is audacious," pronounced Beckwith, after he had skimmed through the last few pages. "Well, Poe, that ends it."

"Ends what?" exclaimed the poet. "Beckwith, I did not endure the Five Points, the Latting Tower, and your Old Jail for this kind of finale. Tell me what is going on or I will take the Haston, shoot you, and read the dossier."

"These papers describe a plan to dismember the United States and return this nation to the British Empire. The plot was contrived by Townshend and supported by Queen Victoria."

"Queen Victoria?" repeated Poe incredulously. "He must have been hopelessly insane to imagine that she would participate in such an intrigue."

"Her Majesty *is* a conspirator in this scheme, and Townshend was far from mad in this respect," Beckwith emphasized. "Actually, it is quite a practical plan. Daring, but workable. So clever, in fact, it is almost foolproof. And the evidence is here, in the Queen's own hand."

Poe reached for the dossier, but Beckwith withdrew it. "There is no time to read it now. Some final details are necessary, so that this affair can be buried. Besides, all the facts are not in this Troy Dossier. I have supplementary information from sources in England and Canada. I will summarize it for you.

"The name Townshend played a vital role in the founding of this nation. It was Charles Townshend who could be credited with having ignited the American Revolution. As Chancellor of the Exchequer, he was responsible for the taxation bill in 1767 which initiated the chain of events leading to the Declaration of Independence. Instability seems a Townshend family trait, for this selfsame man was so erratic that he often spoke against his own faction in Parliament. He was dubbed Champagne Charlie because of his ability to deliver brilliant speeches in the House of Commons while so drunk that he had to be supported by both arms. He died at forty-two of uncertain causes."

Poe hoped that Beckwith would stay put in the chair at the desk, but as expected the Police Superintendent rose and began his infernal pacing.

"Charles had a younger brother, Lewis, who migrated to the colony of New York. He was the father of Richard Townshend. The family acquired considerable land in Manhattan. In fact, we are on part of it now.

"Lewis Townshend was an ardent supporter of the King's cause during the Revolution. However, with the loss of the thirteen colonies, the Townshend land as well as the property of other Loyalists was confiscated. The Townshends fled with other Tory families and resettled in Nova Scotia. Lewis Townshend began his exile in Halifax, and it was this Canadian city which became the headquarters of the United Empire Loyalists, an organization of American colonists who had remained loyal to King George. They hoped that one day the Crown would restore them to the social position and privileges they had enjoyed before the rebellion."

Beckwith held the Troy Dossier in his hands as he continued pacing the room.

"Years went by and, of course, King George could do nothing to restore their American property. Some of the Loyalists returned to the mother country, some became acclimated to their new land, but others became increasingly embittered. Then came a second opportunity, the War of 1812."

"I can surmise the rest," said Poe. "Richard Townshend inherited his hatred of the Americans and eagerly fought against us."

"Precisely, Poe. But it was more than just a war to him, it was vindication. At least, this is what I glean from his writings. Richard Townshend was not only an officer but a Ranger who led war parties of the Six Nations in raids on settlements along the border. Most of these were not battles but massacres. It was his way, I suppose, of tearing out the American presence as he himself had been uprooted. And it became more. For early in his youth, Richard Townshend discovered a dreadful malady within himself. By his own hand, he writes he never revealed it to anyone."

"And that was?"

"He could not have an erection."

"Fate has a way of being cunningly cruel," said Poe. "It must have been galling to him. He appeared masculine in every respect and was a soldier as well as a duelist of renown."

"In addition to this malady, Townshend writes, God heaped another curse upon him. But this part, I think is best told in his own words."

Beckwith read aloud:

"One day, in the year 1814, at the end of a raid, I walked along the edge of a burning Maine settlement waiting for my warriors to reap the harvest of victory. I heard moans from a young girl lying on the ground nearby. Her face was bloodied and her clothes disheveled. It was my intention to end her misery before my Indians scalped her or determine if she could be taken to be one of their squaws. Either way, the fate of an American female was of no great concern. I bent to examine her, and as I did I rubbed against her body. Then for the first time in my life, I had a feeling in my penis. I could not believe it. I pulled her dress down to the waist and felt her breasts and a stiffness came into me. I was astounded. I thought it demeaning, but I had to try it. I lay on top of the semi-conscious girl and the stiffness became more pronounced.

'I pulled her into a cabin and removed her underclothes and my own. As I lay on top of her I felt a surge, an ecstasy I had never felt. Her breathing stopped, but I could not stop. I penetrated her. A wondrous sensation coursed through my body. I stayed within her and I was erect. When I withdrew, I instantly withered.

"This was the end of my affliction, I thought. As soon as I could I engaged one of the camp women, but to no avail. I was as before. On the next raid, after the fighting, I selected a female and

forced myself upon her, but with no results. Then I realized what must be done and with my tomahawk I rendered her unconscious. But this also was not enough. She had to be dying. So to begin the celebration of my manhood I slowly squeezed the breath out of her. As I did, I became a complete man.

"After the fifth time I had done this, I was able to ejaculate. By the ninth time, my excitement was so great that the sperm came merely upon the touch of my penis on the lips of the vagina. It was after that incident that I fully realized the extent of the corruption God had placed upon me: that I, Richard Townshend, was the last of my line. For in the very act of impregnating I would have to destroy that which nourished my seed. Excepting Oedipus, I was the most accursed man ever to have been born. That a man such as myself should be debased generated within me a revulsion. At the source of my contagion, I plunged my knife again and again. But the power of this condemnation had infested my soul. And, as much as I might resist, the urging would come again."

As this recitation ended, a spell of vertigo came upon Poe. "What a grisly tale," the writer commented.

"Townshend had killed at least three more times before he presented himself to the Queen," Beckwith continued. "Peel's investigators uncovered three garrotings, two in Nova Scotia and one in the Westmorland district. Townshend realized that his plan was too important to be jeopardized by his own compulsive behavior. As a safeguard, he decided to disguise himself. The war paint he wore as a Ranger gave him an idea; when he was in London he had learned makeup from a theatrical group. He impersonated you, Poe, because of your unsavory reputation and because the singular garb you wear would be easily recognized. Simultaneously, he would be defaming America's best-known literary personality as the decadent product of this new nation."

The poet clenched his fists. He wished that Townshend were alive so that he might have the opportunity to shoot at him again. This time there would be no temporizing.

"Townshend was ecstatic, not only about going to America to effect his plan but because this trip would make it possible for him to indulge his perverse urge. For this time, instead of random victims, he would select women from the families who had been prominent supporters of the American rebellion, families who, in some cases, were occupying land his father had owned. And he had an available choice in the Literary Liaison. These girls trusted him. Who could ever suspect the British envoy-general of being an insane killer?"

"How could Victoria associate herself with this criminal?" asked an outraged Poe. "Never mind. Evidently she did not know. But how was this plot supposed to work? An English Queen cannot dictate to Parliament."

"For clarity, I think it best to start in general terms," said Beckwith. "The European nations are jealous of our growing power. They resent our Monroe Doctrine, which prohibits further colonization in the New World. Mexico declared war on us, fully expecting European intervention on their side. But it is chiefly to England that we are a constant source of irritation. We have continually coveted Canada and fought two wars in an attempt to obtain it. The English fear our expansion northward as well as westward. It is an open secret that the British government has subsidized the Republic of Texas, hoping it will be a buffer state against American cupidity. The English ambassador has bribed Texan legislators to vote against joining the Union.

"Our country is also the source of arms and money for the cause of Irish independence. So there is considerable antipathy toward America in England as there is a reservoir of hate toward the British in this country.

"To this inflammable situation, add the personality of Victoria: strong-willed, obstinate, prideful, eager to regain the power of the monarchy. What more could cap her reign than restoring the honor of her family with the recovery of America, which George III, her direct forefather, had lost? In the Western Hemisphere, she would be empress of a land stretching from the Arctic

Circle to the Sabine River. Could there be a more appealing prospect to this pompous woman?"

"And exactly how was this to be done?"

"Townshend's plan has two phases. Under the guise of the Queen's inspector of ambassadorial activities, he was to travel this country promoting divisiveness by financing dissident groups. Certainly there are enough of them. He backed the fanatical abolitionists in their antislavery cause. He supported New England's discontent with this Mexican war which that section fears will bring more slave states into the Union. He encouraged Southern extremists, who call for secession rather than abolish slavery. He provided funds to the Know-Nothings, who promote hatred of foreigners. Townshend would promise anything, support any cause which would create discord. It is not too difficult a task, for these days we hardly think of ourselves as Americans, but as Northerners, Southerners, and Westerners, citizens of sovereign states rather than of a nation. After all, Poe, it is only fourteen years since President Jackson threatened to march into South Carolina and hang John Calhoun if nullification by force was attempted. I would say that the situation is worse today.

"Here is an actual case of Townshend's intervention. This is a voucher for a substantial contribution to the campaign of Abraham Lincoln, a Whig, who was elected to the House of Representatives in an area of Illinois normally Democratic. This Lincoln has made a name for himself in Congress as a vociferous opponent of this war."

"And the second phase of Townshend's plan?"

"Military action. The Queen, using her influence, has placed men obedient to her in the War Office and the Admiralty. Illegal orders have been issued outfitting an expedition to invade the United States." Beckwith pulled several orders of battle from the Troy Dossier. "Three squadrons are to rendezvous at staging areas: One is sailing from Halifax to carry a force of United Empire Loyalists to strike Boston, a second flotilla is forming in the mid-Atlantic to invade New York, and a third is to come from the West Indies to hit Charleston. Because of the element of surprise and the fact that our army is fighting in Mexico, there would be little opposition. And on this, the Day of Independence, begins the covert operation. Townshend writes with relish that he allows us this thirty-day period from the Fourth of July to enjoy our last month of independence. August fourth is the day of attack. For his part, he was going to incinerate the city, an idea he got from the Great Fire of 1845. It was to be a diversionary tactic.

"As a reward for the success of this plan, the Queen was to grant him the title Duke of Manhattan and restore the Townshend lands to him—property which would give him a fabulous income, greater than that of John Jacob Astor."

"This is fantastic," the author commented.

"Fantastic but feasible," replied Beckwith. "You see, should this unauthorized force be able to maintain the invasion, the English government would be foolish not to legitimatize the victory by sending its regular forces. If the incursion failed, it would be immaterial if there was no formal proclamation of war. Do you think there would be a way of stopping an Anglo-American conflict at that point? Remember, President Polk ordered our troops to attack the Mexicans before a declaration of war was approved by Congress. Then the full might of the British Empire would come against us. It would be the end of the United States as a nation."

"My God, how can we prevent this?" Poe asked.

"By discreet revelation. This bloody Queen is encroaching on Parliament's power. Once the Troy operation starts, national honor would require the British government to support Victoria's undeclared war. But there is still time for the Prime Minister to rescind spurious orders, recall disloyal or duped officials, and have orders countermanded.

"The fact is, Poe, that this headstrong Queen has always been under surveillance. The Troy correspondence had already aroused suspicion. This is how I was alerted to the situation when I made inquiries about Townshend to Sir Robert Peel. His people knew some intrigue was being planned, but they thought it was directed against their own government. As you know, ever since the 1600s there has been a continual struggle between the monarchy and Parliament for supremacy. I suppose the Queen thought she would recoup the royal power by this venture."

"Now she will be made to abdicate in disgrace," Poe said.

"Not likely," Beckwith predicted. "Revelation of this affair would be an awkward embarrassment to the government. Besides, Victoria has been on the throne for eleven years. She is the symbol of stability of the Empire. If she is forced to abdicate, not only British pride but the English pound would fall. Whatever the outcome she would be safe. That was why the Queen approved Townshend's plan. And as to the morality of this venture, Victoria can sanctimoniously plead that patriotism motivated her."

"Then she should be prosecuted for abetting a murderous criminal," Poe pressed.

"She should be prosecuted for smugness," responded Beckwith.

"What's to be done now?" Poe asked, grateful that his companion had stopped pacing.

"For you, nothing but to accompany me from here," responded his colleague. They hurried downstairs to the bewildered Madelyn. To Poe's chagrin, Beckwith had the effrontery to treat this lady in the most arbitrary manner.

"Madelyn, you must get ready to leave for England. I will arrange passage. Please allow me a few more hours. I will return this afternoon to explain all. I must go now. As you have regard for me, you will do what I ask."

Madelyn twisted the handkerchief in her hand and nodded her assent. The two men went out onto the street. The pavement was wet, for it had started to drizzle.

"And how do you intend to terminate this affair?" asked Poe.

"I am going now to recover Townshend's body. Dr. Reich will certify his death as 'heart failure.' The body will be cremated and the ashes returned to England."

"Along with the Troy Dossier."

"Precisely, Poe. Peel must present proof to his government. And I have decided to take it myself."

"Besides the Troy Dossier, you will be taking Madelyn Townshend."

"I have always wanted to see the land of my forebears. I can think of no pleasanter way to do it."

"Well, you have what you want and I have what I want." The writer smiled.

"What do you mean?"

"I have the greatest journalistic story of the century," the writer declared.

"Poe, you must never utter a word of this to anyone," his companion demanded.

"Are *you* mad, Beckwith? My account will make you a great hero and myself the foremost journalist."

"For the survival of this nation and for the peace of Europe, this affair can never be revealed," articulated Beckwith.

"You would allow that mischievous Queen to get away with treachery?" protested the outraged poet. "And let her sponsorship of a murderous pervert go unpunished? Is hypocrisy the hallmark of your politics?"

"No, but prudence is. There is a point when politics becomes history and history becomes politics. Poe, I trust you. That is why you know about the Troy Dossier. If this plot is exposed, public sentiment could cause war between the United States and England. There is enough hatred on both sides to kindle the conflict. It would be a war our country would lose. This must not happen, for then, even in death, Townshend would have triumphed."

This imposition roiled the poet and he was about to argue further when Beckwith said, "Poe, if you do not remain silent I will fix you as the Garroter and have you committed to an insane asylum where your ravings will go unheeded. Don't force me to do this. I love this country. It has been good to me. I will do anything to prevent the United States from being diminished."

It grated on the writer that he would have to suppress the story, but finally he became convinced that his colleague was right. "I will do as you ask," said Poe.

They turned right onto Beach Street in the direction of St. John's Park. The mistlike summer rain fell steadily.

"My friend," Beckwith said, "I must leave you now. I have many things to do. I will send your money to Fordham village. I also promise you this: On my return from England, if you have been steady, I will see that you obtain an appropriate position."

"Is this patronage because of who I am or to ensure my silence?" asked the poet facetiously.

"What difference does it make?" responded his companion. "Good-bye, Edgar."

"Good-bye, Hollis."

They grasped each other by the hand and walked a few steps arm in arm. Then the Police Sueprintendent hurried on.

"I can surmise from his compulsive personality why Townshend did not kill Sarah Lewissohn," the writer called after him. "Her family had no connection with the Revolution, so for his purpose she was blemished as a sacrifice. But when he had Priscilla Livingston, how did you know that Townshend would be at Hanover Square?"

"I don't know how it was overlooked, but our street names have not been changed since before the Revolution. Townshend had a poetic sense of vengeance. James Rivington was a native New Yorker, but a venomous Tory editor during the British occupation. James DeLancey was another rabid Loyalist, whose huge holdings were expropriated by the Patriots. Both men were evacuated on the same ship as Townshend's father. Whitehall is a group of government buildings in London and the word is now synonymous with the British government. Hanover is the name of the German royal house from which come the present English monarchs. What more appropriate sacrificial altar on the Fourth of July?"

The Police Superintendent looked back. The light from the gas lamp made the drizzle glisten, and the attenuated rays of bluish vapor refracted the poet into corrugated images that filled the street.

"Edgar, study history and know the world."

Just before Beckwith turned the corner, the tenor voice responded from amidst the reflections, so multitudinous that he could not discern the corporeal Poe.

"I prefer my own worlds and my own realities."